"Listen, chief, if you plan to threaten me every step of the way, then I won't touch you and you can bleed to death."

He pushed her aside and tried to stand. His legs wobbled and his head spun. She coaxed him back to the sofa.

"Save it. I've had enough of your attitude."

She tore the shirt away from his body and he hissed with the burn. When her fingers grazed his skin he thought he'd scream. Gentle, tender touches he couldn't remember feeling from a woman.

Steam rose from the bowl of water. She wrung out the washcloth and reached out. Her eyes were brilliant green with fiery hints of amber. She patted around the exit wound, and her pained expression puzzled him. She scrunched up her nose as if she'd been the one shot and was suffering the pain of a cleansing. He hardly felt her touch when she swabbed the area with ointment.

"What's the verdict?" he asked.

"You'll live." She sounded disappointed. "Lean forward so I can clean the other side."

He followed her order, the gun dangling from his hand.

"I hate guns," she muttered, softly brushing the cotton cloth against his skin. "To think what they can do to a man."

"Or a woman."

PAT WHITE

LOVING THE ENEMY

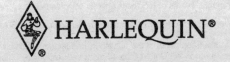

HARLEQUIN®

TORONTO • NEW YORK • LONDON
AMSTERDAM • PARIS • SYDNEY • HAMBURG
STOCKHOLM • ATHENS • TOKYO • MILAN • MADRID
PRAGUE • WARSAW • BUDAPEST • AUCKLAND

To the ladies of Chicago North RWA for their knowledge, wisdom and encouragement.

ISBN-13: 978-0-373-69325-2
ISBN-10:   0-373-69325-7

LOVING THE ENEMY

Copyright © 2008 by Pat White

ABOUT THE AUTHOR

Growing up in the Midwest, Pat White has been spinning stories in her head ever since she was a little girl—stories filled with mystery, romance and adventure. Years later, while trying to solve the mysteries of raising a family in a house full of men, she started writing romance fiction. After six Golden Heart nominations and a *Romantic Times BOOKreviews* Award for Best Contemporary Romance (2004), her passion for storytelling and love of a good romance continues to find a voice in her tales of romantic suspense. Pat now lives in the Pacific Northwest and she's still trying to solve the mysteries of living in a house full of men—with the added complication of two silly dogs and three spoiled cats. She loves to hear from readers, so please visit her at www.patwhitebooks.com.

Books by Pat White

HARLEQUIN INTRIGUE

944—SILENT MEMORIES
968—THE AMERICAN TEMP AND THE BRITISH INSPECTOR*
974—THE ENGLISH DETECTIVE AND THE ROOKIE AGENT*
980—MISS FAIRMONT AND THE GENTLEMAN
  INVESTIGATOR*
1038—SOLDIER SURRENDER
1058—LOVING THE ENEMY

*The Blackwell Group

CAST OF CHARACTERS

Andrea Franks—Young widow who hides from her husband's shame in the Rocky Mountains. Unfortunately, three years after Jimmy's death, his grisly past comes calling.

Kyle McKendrick—A Beta Force operative on the run, Kyle is determined to find the evidence to destroy his superior officer who turned the team into ruthless assassins.

Major Biehl—Creator of Beta Force and an egomaniac who's determined to destroy anyone who threatens his power.

Lieutenant Crane—Friend or enemy? Kyle could use an ally when caught by Crane and Biehl's death squad.

Henry Simpson—Local friend who wants to help Andrea escape the enemy, but is it too late?

Chapter One

Andrea Franks took a deep breath and struggled to seem unaffected by her enemy's presence.

"You shouldn't have come," she said.

"I have to talk to you." The middle-aged military man stood over her, casting a shadow across her sacred space.

Sitting cross-legged on the solid earth she continued to focus on Sparrow Lake, fed by run-off from the snow-capped Rocky Mountains. The lake water rippled in soft, calm waves, so unlike the rage building in her chest. The evil was back, invading her precious serenity.

"I want you off my property," she said.

"Not until we talk."

Daisy and Oscar growled, her golden retrievers in tune to their master's mood.

"I have nothing to say to you, Biehl." Major Thaddeus Biehl, the devil who had led her husband directly into hell.

She took another deep breath, hoping that if she ignored him he'd disappear as quickly as he'd come.

"I'm not leaving until you hear me out."

She straightened to her full five foot eight inches. Adjusting the belt of her beige cotton tunic, she faced the man who had destroyed all that she'd held dear. "You promised never to find me, not to make contact. You've invaded my privacy and I resent it." She plucked her pillow and dried sage from the ground as casually as she could.

"Can you fault me for wanting to check on an old friend?"

"Friend?" She brushed past him and started up the trail toward the cabin. "Now that's a joke."

Determined male footsteps disturbed the slumber of mountain animals as Major Biehl closed the distance between them.

"Wait." He touched her shoulder.

Chills shot down her spine. She glared at his well-manicured fingers then looked into his cool gray eyes. Eyes devoid of honor, eyes devoid of a soul.

Oscar growled a warning, complete with bared teeth.

Biehl let his hand slip from her shoulder. "Something's happened."

She waited, stripping her countenance of every possible emotion. She'd become a master at hiding her thoughts and feelings. At times, even from herself.

"One of our operatives has disappeared from our hospital in Denver," he said.

"More like escaped from your prison." She had her suspicions about what happened to operatives who developed a conscience after discovering the truth about Beta Force.

"We think he's coming this way." His expression softened.

She'd only met Biehl twice in her life: the first time when Jimmy had brought him home, excited about what Biehl was offering, and the second when Biehl had told her about Jimmy's death.

And the worst part was, she hadn't felt much of anything when she'd heard the news. Jimmy had seemed dead to her long before he was killed in the line of "duty."

Guilt settled low in her belly.

"I've come to ask for your help," Biehl said.

"My help?" She squeezed the satchel of dried herbs in a vice-like grip. "How can I possibly help you?"

"You know the terrain better than anyone." He motioned with his hand toward the mountains. "You could help us track him."

"No, thank you."

"Then how about we set up a mobile unit in your cabin? I'm sure there's plenty of room." He eyed her home with devouring eyes.

She fisted her hand to keep from slapping his face back to attention. He had no right looking at the cabin that way. No right at all. Wasn't it enough that he'd stripped her husband of his honor and integrity? Now he wanted to strip Andrea of her new, safe life as well?

"I can't help you," she said.

He sighed. "Andrea, Jimmy would have wanted—"

"How could you possibly know what he wanted? I was married to him for seven years and hadn't a clue who he really was."

Biehl pulled out a cigarette and struck a match. His cheeks hollowed with the first, long drag of tobacco. "Surely you feel some loyalty to the organization considering everything we've done for you?"

Like turn her husband into a killer?

"Jimmy is gone. That part of my life is over."

If only that were true. Her isolated existence proved otherwise. She turned and walked away.

"Wait a minute. We're not done," he said.

Get to the cabin. Lock the door. Forget the past.

"I've got work to do," she shot over her shoulder.

"Like what? Plant more weeds? Honestly, Andy, you'd think you had a full day's work ahead of you."

She spun around and squared off at him. "You have no idea what my days are like. You and your country-club memberships, your wife and two kids in the suburbs. Does your wife have any idea what you really do for a living?"

He exhaled gray smoke and narrowed his eyes.

"I didn't think so," she said. "And don't ever call me Andy."

She marched to the wooden stairs of her log cabin, the dogs trotting beside her.

"I need you to hear me out."

Pausing at the foot of the stairs, she removed the elastic hair band from her wrist. In quick, short jerks, she secured her long, black hair into a ponytail. She always wore her hair free during meditation. It helped her feel open and at peace.

That peace was now shattered by ghosts of the past. She'd been a fool to think she'd ever be free of them.

She turned to face him. "Make your speech and go."

He crossed his arms over his chest. "We need to find this man before he does something stupid."

"Like realize his sins?"

He glared. She swallowed down her next retort. The man had the power to shoot her and call it his national duty. They both knew it.

"You can help us," he said. "I could have a team here in twenty-four hours."

"How dare you threaten to take my home away from me after everything you've done."

"I gave Jimmy an opportunity to fulfill a dream."

"Stop, just stop talking." Because if he didn't, she was going to haul off and slap him.

"Andrea, you're not safe out here." He paused. "Alone."

Sure, she wasn't safe from people like him.

"I would hate it if something happened to you because of one of my agents," he added in a caring tone.

"I can take care of myself."

"I'm sure you can. But honor dictates I protect my men and their families. I heard Jimmy's brother and his wife had a baby boy about a year and a half ago. What does that make, two kids now?"

Regret tore through her at the mention of her nephew, hers and Jimmy's namesake. Another child she would never know.

"Andrew James. They call him A.J.," she whispered.

She'd only seen the child once and it had nearly torn her apart. Being around the love, the warmth of Jimmy's family only intensified her pain as she clung to the truth she'd never be able to share with them. They deserved to remember Jimmy as a hero.

"**Andrew** James," Biehl repeated. "Must be nearing the **terrible** twos. Toddlers can get into all kinds of trouble at that age."

"**Excuse** me? Is that a threat?"

"**A threat?** God, no, Andrea, what do you think I am?" He **smiled** again. Her blood ran cold.

"**I want to** protect you," he said. "For my own peace of mind, I'll leave a radio with you. It's tuned in to our frequency so if you see anything strange you can contact me immediately. This soldier is an expert at jungle warfare. I'd hate to see you come up against him by accident. He's extremely dangerous."

"How dangerous?"

"He's killed people."

She laughed, a deep, throaty sound unfamiliar to even herself. "And this surprises you? What did you pay him to do? Dress up as Santa Claus and do the malls at Christmas?"

His jaw twitched. "You know what I mean. He's killed the wrong people."

"Killing is killing. There's no right or wrong way to kill."

"Anyway," he flicked a bug off the wooden rail, "it's in your best interest to help us. I'm sure you'll come to realize that." He went to his Jeep and pulled a hand-held radio from the front seat. He held it out to her and she just stared at the black device. He placed it on the stairs beside her.

He started back to his car, then turned to smile at her. "Good seeing you again." His gaze raked across her body.

She stood straight. She would not be intimidated by this bastard. "Good-bye, Major."

He settled himself behind the wheel of his car, glanced in the rearview mirror and smoothed his salt-and-pepper hair into place. He shot her a smile, a smile of knowing, a smile of death.

The government-issued vehicle kicked into gear and groaned its way up the steep gravel drive. She wished for a torrential rain to wash away all roads leading to her private sanctuary.

Biehl disappeared beyond a cluster of spruce trees, out of sight, but not out of her life.

Never out of her life.

"Damn it!" she cried, racing up the stairs and swinging open the cabin door. The dogs ran past her to claim the ideal spot under the kitchen table. She slammed the door and stormed toward the bedroom, frustration blurring her vision.

She'd eluded them for three years, enough time to start the healing and plant the seeds of hope. But they were back, wrapping her in the palm of their iron fist and squeezing with firm, agonizing pressure. She knew the depth of Biehl's power. No one could help her.

Since Jimmy's death she'd made it her goal not to need anyone's help, especially a man's, nor would she be pushed around by one.

Now Biehl was threatening the most remote connection she had to another living soul: her nephew. An innocent child. That's what he was doing, wasn't it? Mentioning A.J. in the same breath as getting into trouble? Or was she being paranoid?

"I've got to warn them," she said, determined to protect the little boy. She'd have to call her brother-in-law. And say what? She'd never told Jimmy's family the truth about his role in Beta Force. It would tear them apart to know he was a killer, not a hero.

She went into the bedroom, ripping her cotton tunic as she stripped it off. She opened the top drawer of the oak chest and groped for something to wear.

Nothing seemed right. She was a fool to think it would ever be right again. She pulled open the bottom drawer and dug into the pile of soft cotton pants. Her fingers hit glass and her breath caught.

She cupped the silver picture frame, pulled it from the drawer and read the engraved words: Andrea and James, Loving a Lifetime 1998.

Two strangers stared back at her: a girl of twenty-one with feathered bangs and a young man with white-blond hair, cut in military style. She'd forgotten how handsome he was, perfect white teeth gleaming with what they used to call his "million-dollar smile." And his eyes. She'd once confessed her fear of drowning in the clarity of his pure blue eyes.

Andy and Jimmy. The perfect couple. Everyone thought they'd live happily ever after. They couldn't imagine the secrets that would destroy them.

"Jimmy," she whispered, eyeing the photograph of the boy named most likely to succeed where everyone else failed. He was a hard-working student, a natural athlete and a loyal son.

A trusting soul who believed in people.

Pain swelling in her chest, she hurled the photograph against the wall, the glass splintering like a spider's web. Then her eyes caught on something else. Jimmy's diary. She pulled the maroon leather book from her drawer and clutched it to her chest. The government letter recognizing his brave service stuck out between the pages.

"Oh, Jimmy," she whispered. She hadn't been able to bring herself to read his diary. Yet it brought her peace to have this part of him.

Hugging her knees to her chest, she willed away the tears. She thought she'd created an impregnable shield to protect her from her grief.

Tonight the feelings came rushing back: helplessness and grief, pain she thought might keep her from breathing.

"No," she said. Biehl's threats would not consume her. She'd find a way to protect her family and fight the evil that had obliterated her life once before. This time she would not be a victim.

BREATHE, DAMMIT. Block out the pain.

Kyle McKendrick focused on those thoughts, determined to stay alive. If only he could outmaneuver the soldiers and disappear into the mountains. He glanced at the towering trees and thanked God he'd made it this far.

Taking another step, he stumbled into a tree, the pain shooting down his arm to his fingertips. He leaned against the tree for support, but his knees buckled. Giving in, just for a second, he sat down and closed his eyes in surrender.

Get up! Only a punk would give up now! Stand at attention, soldier!

He inhaled the crisp scent of pine and fought the pain caused by a well-aimed bullet. In reality, the pain had begun the day he'd joined Beta Force.

His thoughts wandered as he slid his hand inside the leather jacket he'd swiped from an unsuspecting tourist. Squeezing his shoulder, he hoped the wound had finally started to clot. Instead, warmth spread across his hand. Fresh blood. He clamped his hand tighter against the wound and tipped his head back.

How had it gotten so out of control? All he'd wanted to do was help people, save lives.

Instead he'd ended up taking the life of his best friend.

Jimmy. Guilt arced through his chest, intensifying the pain of his shoulder wound.

Can't think about that now. Have to find her, get the evidence and put Biehl away.

And then?

Panic hovered low. Damn drugs. Biehl's mad scientists had taken special care to use anxiety-inducing meds to try and terrorize the information out of Kyle.

But there was nothing more horrific than killing your best friend. Neither drugs nor torture would prevent Kyle from making that right and putting Biehl behind bars.

And nothing would absolve Kyle of his sin.

A mountain lion cried out. He wondered what would get him first; wild animals or Beta Force? Did it matter? If he died, his mission died with him.

You can't let that happen.

He pushed forward, figuring that Beta Force agents were everywhere, including in the local hospitals. Biehl had probably notified law enforcement with some bull story about an escaped psychotic killer, hoping Kyle would be shot on sight.

He couldn't be shot, not before he found the evidence that would destroy Major Biehl and his death army.

It was a damned miracle Kyle could think straight with all the drugs they'd pumped into him. He hoped his brain hadn't failed him, he hoped he was heading in the right direction—toward a cabin inhabited by a woman who had evidence against Biehl. Kyle didn't know who she was and he didn't care. As long as she gave up the evidence.

Edging upwards against the tree, he took a steadying breath. He aimed toward the sound of a barking dog through the thick mass of pine. Squinting to see through the darkness he spotted a cabin, smoke floating from the chimney. He got closer, pressing his hand to his wound, and spied through an open cabin window.

A tall, slender woman, maybe in her early thirties, threw clothes violently around her bedroom, shouting at someone, he guessed a companion. But as he peered through each window he realized she was alone. Sitting on the bed, she hugged her knees to her chest, her long, dark hair spread across her shoulders like a cocoon of protection. As she rocked slightly, she was a vision of beauty…and vulnerability.

This was not the time to feel compassion. It would only cloud his judgment. This woman fitted the description his contact had given him.

Muted saxophone music drifted from an open window. He edged closer to the house and peered inside. He could see everything from this vantage point, including clear jars of beans and pastas lining the countertop, plants on the kitchen windowsill and wood burning in the living-room fireplace. A golden retriever lay curled up beside it.

The home radiated warmth, serenity and peace.

Peace he'd have to destroy to save himself and complete his mission.

Suddenly, a larger retriever raced to the window and barked at Kyle. He crouched down and held his breath. Too late to run for cover.

The woman commanded the dog to stop barking, and she squinted to look outside. Kyle could tell she was blinded by the darkness, yet he could see plenty: an enchantress with jet-black hair, wearing a cotton wrap that hinted at generous curves. She jerked the curtains closed.

Yet through a crack in the curtains he watched her amble into the bathroom, hands cradling her face. The larger golden retriever followed her, while the other dog stretched and yawned, retreating under the kitchen table.

Kyle shoved his hands into the pockets of the leather coat and struggled to focus against the pain, his skin burning as if seared by a cattle iron. He needed relief and needed it fast. Gauze and painkillers would work. A fifth of Jack Daniel's would be even better.

First he had to get the dogs out of the cabin. Hell, he'd created plenty of distractions that kept the federales occupied while he zipped in, took care of business, and zipped back out without anyone being the wiser.

Devising a plan, he walked to the front of the house and hesitated at the sight of a communications radio sitting on the stairs.

Not only was she one of them, but a sloppy agent as well. Biehl must have assigned her to keep an eye on things west of Denver.

He fingered the cold steel of the Glock tucked into the waist of his jeans. The gun would convince the woman to cooperate and tell him what she knew about Biehl's plans for renegade agent, Kyle McKendrick. He didn't have to stretch his imagination for that one.

Torture followed by death.

He slipped under the stairs for cover. He could cut the power and go in. No, that was bold and stupid considering his physical condition. He'd wait for her to settle in for the night, then make his move. Kyle was considered one of the best at what he did, not that he took pride in that fact.

Focusing on blocking out his pain, his thoughts drifted to the earlier days of his youth. He'd always craved excitement and adventure.

And respect.

Those needs had led him into the army, a tour in Iraq and recruitment into Beta Force—a team that was completely off the government's radar.

Damn, why had he been so gullible? So gullible that he'd convinced Jimmy to join as well?

Kyle's need for respect had led him into the deceitful hands of Biehl and his gruesome missions. Biehl had used Kyle as a weapon against people who were not his enemies…

He started to drift, struggling to stay conscious. Maybe he'd lost too much blood and his body wasn't strong enough to finish this.

Had to focus on something, anything. He thought about his high-school girlfriend. She'd had long black hair too, like the woman inside. Jenny was sweet and kind and had always believed in Kyle. He remembered the sparkle in her blue eyes, the softness of her pale cheeks—

The sound of a woman's cry made him jump. He bolted upright, disoriented. A bright fire crackled a hundred feet away. The woman from the cabin stood outside by the fire, her arms raised to the heavens, her voice calling out to the sky. She wore a loose-fitting jacket over a baggy shirt and cotton pants. Her feet were bare and her hair fell halfway down her back. She pulled a piece of clothing from a black bag and tossed it into the fire. Then another. The dogs barked from inside the cabin.

Perfect. This was his chance.

He stood and plastered himself against the house for support. The fire threw shadows across the mountains, shadows that took the shape of monsters and demons. Fatigue threatened to swallow him as he watched the woman's agonized ritual. She tossed the bag into the fire and dropped to her knees, her arms wrapped around her midsection.

The fire burned his cheeks as he closed in on the bewitching beauty. He wondered how she could stand the heat. He strained to focus on the woman who sat very still and stared into the fire.

"You're him, aren't you?" she said, not turning around. Her voice startled him, husky yet feminine. "You're the man they're looking for."

He pressed the gun barrel to the back of her head. She didn't flinch.

"Now, why would anybody be looking for me?"

"He didn't tell me why."

"C'mon." He tapped the gun barrel against her head. "Let's go inside."

"No one comes inside. Not even a man with a gun."

The chill in her voice set him on edge. He didn't want to kill her. He'd tasted enough death to last him five lifetimes.

"Is that right?" He still had enough use of his fingers to grab a fistful of hair and tug. "Let's go."

She stood, seemingly immune to his grip, and he steered them toward the cabin. With one hand in her hair and the other clutching the Glock, he followed her up the stairs. She was tall for a woman, yet her features were incredibly feminine. Her hair was smooth and her scent erotically appealing. He gave himself a mental shake. It had been too long since he'd been with a woman. He wasn't about to lose his life to this one. As they approached the landing he noticed how she walked with the quiet step of an Indian, soft and graceful.

With an ear-piercing cry, she elbowed him in the stomach. Startled, he let go of her hair. She spun around and kneed him in the groin.

Stars flashed across his vision as he fell to his knees. She kicked him in his wounded shoulder. He tumbled down the stairs, catching glimpses of his life with each bump. The woman would probably kill him before he hit the ground.

He jerked to a stop, his head slamming against the unforgiving earth. Sprawled on his back he could feel blood ooze from his shoulder wound. He caught a glimpse of her horrified expression. Why? This couldn't be the first time she'd seen blood—or shed it.

She disappeared into the house, probably to get her weapon. He surrendered to the blackness, praying to God that he wasn't the only one who knew the truth about Beta Force and begging forgiveness for not surviving long enough to destroy it.

Chapter Two

"Damn you!" Andrea cried, slamming the door and pounding on it with closed fists.

Her attacker, although temporarily indisposed, would regain consciousness and come after her again. She raced to the front closet, nearly tripping over the dogs as they pranced around her legs. She pulled out the black case that had been delivered with Jimmy's things. She'd sent most of his personal items to his brother, but this she'd kept as a reminder never to trust again.

And now she might have to use it.

Kneeling on the hardwood floor, she flipped open the case. Her breath caught in her throat. The shiny pistol taunted her, a gun used to kill how many people?

With trembling fingers she gripped the weapon. Her life depended on having the courage to kill a man. The metal weighed heavy in her palm, and even heavier on her soul.

She believed in peace, compassion and the goodness of the human spirit. She'd thought her husband had shared her beliefs. Only upon his death had she discovered the truth.

"I can't become a part of this." She put the gun back in the case. There had to be another way. She'd call Biehl. After all, it was his agent threatening her life.

The thought twisted her stomach into knots. To think she'd consider going to that heinous group for help.

No. She'd run. Andrea was good at running. The agent would never find her if she disappeared among the pine and aspen of the Rockies.

Running again. She sounded like a coward.

What she needed most was time to think. She scrambled through the cabin, turning off the lights to put the agent at a disadvantage. It was so quiet outside.

Carefully unlocking the front door, she peered through the crack. The dying flames cast shadows across the man sprawled at the foot of the stairs.

She didn't understand. Operatives were made of tougher stuff than that. A tumble down the stairs shouldn't have rendered him unconscious, unless he'd broken his neck in the fall. She closed the door and pressed her forehead to the smooth wood.

"He threatened you," she told herself. "Don't you dare feel sorry for him."

But it was in her nature to heal the wounded. She'd tried to heal Jimmy's spirit over and over again, each time losing a part of herself as he pushed her further away.

"This has nothing to do with Jimmy." She turned to the dogs. "Who am I kidding?"

Everything she felt and did was a result of Jimmy's betrayal. Thanks to Jimmy, the shadow of Biehl and his army of murderers would follow her indefinitely. Unless...

Unless she gave Biehl the man lying outside her cabin.

The dogs burst into a chorus of barks. They must have sensed the agent approaching the door. She grabbed the gun, balancing the cool metal between her shaky fingers.

"I have to do this," she said, aiming it at the door. She struggled to steady her trembling hands.

The piercing cry of a mountain lion shot a chill down her spine. It wasn't the agent that had excited the dogs, but a wild cat on the prowl.

"Shush," she said, huddling by the door with them. Oscar growled beside her ear.

"Don't even think about it, Studly," she warned.

Another sharp cry echoed through her front window. What if dinner was the unconscious agent lying at the base of her stairs?

"Good, then he won't be my problem anymore." The image of his body being torn to pieces shot a wave of guilt through her chest.

Wasn't she as bad as Beta Force if she let him die like that?

The cat cried out again, and she wondered if the agent had regained consciousness and had threatened the animal.

"Tough," she said. She shouldn't have an ounce of sympathy for the man.

She cracked open the door and peered outside. The agent seemed to be unconscious. Another cry echoed from a small cluster of trees beyond the house. The mountain lion was stalking its prey from the darkness.

"Get up," she whispered.

Had Jimmy ever been this vulnerable while on a mission? Had a stranger ever helped him fight off his enemies lurking out of sight?

She wrapped her fingers around the butt of the gun. She couldn't kill an animal, but hoped a few warning shots would discourage the cat.

"I can't believe I'm doing this," she said, clutching the firearm. She abhorred guns, yet was about to fire one to save her enemy's life.

She couldn't help herself. Deep in her core she was a healer.

Releasing the safety, she wrapped her fingers around the pistol grip and prayed for a miracle so she wouldn't have to do this. Another shrill cry made her jump. She stepped out onto the landing, ordering the dogs to stay inside.

The agent stood, gripping his left shoulder. He swayed and nearly dropped again, but regained his balance. If she didn't know better she'd think he was trying to challenge the cat. Either that, or he had a death wish.

The lion slipped out of the darkness and paced back and forth along the perimeter of the tree-lined property. The cat snarled, his sharp white teeth gleaming in the moonlight.

"You want a part of me? C'mon!" the agent cried, then stumbled, but didn't fall.

A high-pitched cry from the mountain lion shot adrenaline to her fingertips. She closed her eyes and squeezed the trigger three times. Bile rose in her throat. The cat jetted off.

The man looked at her, then toward the trees where the lion had disappeared. As if realizing his reprieve, he dropped to one knee.

This was it, her chance to get to the radio at the foot

of the stairs and call for help. Daisy pushed past her and raced toward the man.

"Daisy, no!" she called, afraid he still had enough fight in him to hurt the dog. Daisy ran up to the man and nudged the arm that held him up.

The agent collapsed. The dog sniffed him like a panicked mother fretting over an injured pup.

Andrea ran down the stairs, still clutching the gun. The dog nudged at the man's shoulder but he didn't move, didn't make a sound.

Daisy barked repeatedly.

"What is it, girl?" she said.

"It's a gunshot wound from a nine-millimeter Glock."

She was startled by the sound of his deep, hoarse voice. His eyes remained closed and sweat beaded on his forehead.

"I thought you were unconscious," she said.

He cracked open his dark brown eyes. "Didn't want to miss being the main course at my own funeral feast. You're a pretty bad shot." He eyed Jimmy's gun.

"I wasn't trying to kill him. Just scare him away. I could never kill anything."

"Sure, babe. Whatever you say."

KYLE CLOSED his eyes. Great. Not only had he been captured by one of Biehl's agents, but she was wacky as hell. Never kill anything? Who was she kidding?

"Let's get you inside before he comes back." She pushed aside the golden retriever, who anxiously sniffed at Kyle's injury. "Okay, girl." She patted the dog's head.

The woman crouched down and his nostrils filled

with the sweet scent of her, some kind of wildflower. He studied her round eyes, a shade of green richer than the tree-covered mountains. He felt himself drawn to their earthy color.

Then he noticed the gun lying on the ground beside her. A short reach and he could be back on top. Unfortunately he'd have to grab it with his left hand and that was on fire at the moment.

"Slowly, you can do it. Take a deep breath," the woman coached.

A typical operative wouldn't have saved him from a wild animal attack and wouldn't be helping him with the compassion of a nurse. Then again, Biehl needed Kyle alive. Placing his arm around her shoulder, she steered him toward the cabin.

"What about your gun?" he said. *Careless* didn't begin to describe this agent.

"Oh, yeah." She grabbed the gun and shoved it into her jacket pocket.

Her steadiness surprised him. He naturally leaned away from the pain and into her strength.

"We're almost there," she said. "Just a few more steps. Is it bleeding a lot?"

"I'm not sure." He wasn't fooled by her false concern.

When they neared the cabin door the bigger of the two dogs blocked the steps and barked.

"Oscar, hush. It's okay," she said.

The golden retriever didn't budge.

"I said knock it off! Heel."

The dog growled at Kyle, then went to her side.

"He doesn't like me," he said.

"He's protective. I don't let many people into the cabin."

"I know. Not even a man with a gun."

She cleared her throat as if embarrassed by her earlier declaration. They walked past the radio and climbed the stairs. She wasn't bringing it inside? Interesting.

She led him into the cabin and the glint of shiny pistol steel caught his eye, taunting him to go for it.

But the encounter with the mountain lion had sapped his energy. He'd never felt so vulnerable in his life. As a Beta Force agent, she'd have him drugged and tied up like a tom turkey in minutes: a perfect feast for his old friend, Major Biehl.

The dog she called Daisy raced across the living room, but Oscar stayed close to his mistress. Smart dog. He knew what Kyle was thinking.

She turned on another lamp and he grabbed her wrist. "Don't. We're wide open with the lights on."

"What difference does a little light make?"

She stared at him with those enchanting green eyes. Innocent and questioning eyes. She was better than good. She was damned near convincing.

"Just…don't," he said.

She shrugged and took off her jacket, laying it over a kitchen chair. He bit back a moan as he collapsed against the thick-cushioned sofa.

"Let's see what we've got here." She went to him and slipped her hand between his jacket and the gunshot wound. He squeezed his eyes shut.

"It's okay. It's done," she whispered.

He could hardly believe it. Somehow she'd detached the lining of the jacket from the sticky wound, and with little pain. Fatigue grabbed hold of his thoughts. It had been a hellish week wandering the countryside with no money, food or friends to rely on. Then he'd been nailed by Biehl's sharpshooter and thought it was over.

"We need to get your jacket and shirt off to cleanse the wound," she said.

He leaned forward, but kept her clearly in his peripheral vision. She peeled the jacket from his left arm, then his right, and tossed it aside.

"Now the shirt." She hesitated. "Great. You would be wearing a pullover. I'm going to have to cut it off you. Unless you think you can raise that arm above your head."

"Cut it off," he rasped, disgusted by his own weakness.

Standing, she banged her knee against the edge of the coffee table. "Argh! I can't see a damned thing."

She flipped on one lamp, then another, each time growing more irritated. Why was she so angry? She should know better than to expose herself to the enemy.

Wait a minute. She *was* the enemy.

She reached for something in the front closet and came at him carrying a dark bag. Panic flooded his chest. Her job was to gain his trust, subdue him and rip open his soul. He mustered his last bit of strength, grabbed her wrist and hauled her down on the couch, pinning her with his body. The dog growled by his ear.

"Tell the dog to back off or I swear, I'll kill him after I strangle you."

"Oscar, sit." She stared defiantly into Kyle's eyes. "Now, get off me."

"Biehl won't get me that easy. The gun," he demanded.

"What about it?"

"I need it."

"It's in my jacket pocket on the kitchen chair," she ground out.

He got up and pulled her with him for protection against the dog. The other golden perked her ears and looked at Kyle but didn't budge from under the table.

They edged toward the chair. Holding her wrist with his good hand, he gingerly searched the pocket. His nearly numb fingers grabbed the gun, and he shifted it into his good hand.

"Feel better now?" she said. "Sit down so I can dress your wound."

She walked away from him as if he wasn't threatening her with a gun, as if tending his wound was her primary objective.

He knew better.

Struggling to stay focused he sat down on the couch. When he glanced up, she was coming at him with something pointed in her hand. He raised the gun, aiming the barrel at her chest.

She glared. "Listen, chief, if you plan to threaten me every step of the way then I won't help you and you can bleed to death."

"What have you got there?"

"Scissors. Your shirt, remember? Unless you've got a burning desire to lift that left arm so I can pull it off."

He ground his teeth. He could barely raise the limp arm off his lap.

"I didn't think so," she said. "I'll make you a deal. The minute you feel me go for your heart with these four-inch scissors, you shoot. Okay?" She flicked the scissors twice, acting like she was talking to a child.

"Listen, lady—"

"Save it. I've had enough people give me attitude today."

"Who else has been here?"

"Biehl, of course."

"Biehl was here? Hell, I've gotta go." He pushed her aside and tried to stand. His legs wobbled and his head spun. She coaxed him back to the sofa.

"You're not going anywhere." She reached into her bag.

Damn, she could pull any number of weapons out of there.

"Let me see what you've got." He squinted against the dizziness filling his head and flicked the gun barrel sideways.

She turned the bag upside down, emptying the contents on the couch. No hypodermic needles or pills, just gauze, tape, bottles with pictures of flowers on them and jars of ointment.

"I'm trying to help," she said.

"Whatever. I keep the gun."

Shaking her head, she pulled his shirt from the waistband of his jeans. She carefully snipped away, cutting a line straight up the center. When her fingers grazed his skin he thought he'd scream. Gentle, tender touches he couldn't remember feeling from a woman.

Touches of sympathy, touches of compassion.

Impossible. This woman couldn't be feeling anything but resentment toward him, the man who'd threatened her after she'd saved him from the salivating mountain lion. The drugs had truly destroyed his good sense.

"There." She spread the two halves of his shirt aside and glanced at his chest, then up into his eyes.

This strong, brazen woman actually blushed.

"Um, this is the tricky part. We need the shirt completely off so I can secure the bandage. Deep breathing," she coached, and slowly pulled at the blood-encrusted shirt. Such care and compassion filled her eyes.

It nearly had him believing…

No, he wouldn't be seduced by a clever agent, even with only half of his brain working.

"Just rip the damn thing off," he said.

She tore the shirt away from his body and he clenched his teeth against the sting.

"I need to get a washcloth." She stood.

"Stay where I can see you."

Ignoring his order, she disappeared into the bathroom. He tensed. She could pull a twelve-gauge shotgun out of the bathtub and blow him away.

A minute later she walked toward him, a washcloth and small bowl in her hands. She sat down and fiddled with the supplies she'd dumped on the couch. Steam rose from the bowl of water as she wrung out the washcloth and reached out. He automatically jerked back.

"It's water and a mild cleansing solution," she explained. "What do you think I'm going to do to you?"

He looked at the cloth, then into her eyes, brilliant green with fiery hints of amber. He read truth in her eyes and he wanted to kick himself for being so gullible.

The fact was, his wound burned all the way to his fingertips. If left untreated he could die from infection.

"You know what you're doing?" he asked.

"Like you're in any position to be picky?"

No, he wasn't. He was completely at her mercy. He nodded for her to continue. She patted around the exit wound and her pained expression puzzled him. She scrunched up her nose as if she'd been the one shot. He hardly felt her touch when she swabbed the area with ointment. Then again, his shoulder might be completely numb due to infection.

"What's the verdict?" he asked.

"You'll live." She sounded disappointed. "Lean forward so I can clean the other side."

He followed her order, the gun dangling from his hand. Heaviness pressed against his eyelids as she patted and stroked, murmuring words of comfort. Unbelievable. He clutched a gun in his hand and she still soothed him with her voice. If she wasn't a nurse she must be an angel. He'd never been treated with such tenderness, and he'd been in and out of hospitals more times than he cared to admit.

What the hell was the matter with him? She was working him by earning his trust. His instincts must have been completely scrambled by the drugs. The major had met his objective. Kyle nearly let his guard slip thinking maybe he'd stumbled upon a guardian angel.

"I hate guns," she muttered, softly brushing the cotton cloth against his skin. "To think what they can do to a man."

"Or a woman."

Sitting back on the sofa, she dropped the bloodied cloth into the bowl of water.

"I should have let that lion tear you apart." Standing, she tossed the gauze and tape to the couch. "Bandage yourself. Take anything you want—food, money." She grabbed a ceramic jar off the kitchen counter and plucked tens and twenties from it. She littered the coffee table with the cash. "Take it. I don't care. Just be gone by morning."

She marched toward the bedroom, Oscar close behind.

"Wait a minute," he said, struggling to grip the gun, but the buzzing filled his head, making it impossible to focus.

She turned and glanced across the living room at the second golden retriever. "Daisy, come!"

The dog lifted her head, but didn't move from her spot under the kitchen table.

"Daisy!"

The mutt laid her head down between outstretched paws.

"Fine." The woman slammed the bedroom door.

His head spun and his shoulder throbbed. He had to get her back into the living room and tie her up. But how? Threaten her dog? He glanced at the lazy mutt and couldn't help but smile. Beta Force might have turned him into a killer but they couldn't destroy his love of animals.

He glanced at the bedroom door. He didn't trust her, no matter how caring she'd been while tending his wound. He couldn't trust anybody, not with Biehl so close.

He dropped the gun on the sofa then fingered the medical supplies she'd dumped in his lap. He hadn't a clue what to put on his wound.

"Hell." He struggled to slice off a piece of tape with the scissors. His vision blurred and his fingers trembled like an alcoholic in detox.

He dropped the scissors and leaned back against the sofa. His thoughts drifted to that place that sucked him down whenever unconsciousness hovered close by.

He heard Jimmy's voice calling his name, "Mac, don't leave me!"

Leave no man behind. His best friend—they were leaving Jimmy. Biehl's order because Jimmy had betrayed him.

Have to go back, save Jimmy.

As the chopper hovered, the terrorists dragged Jimmy into the middle of camp.

Dizzy, Kyle struggled to stay conscious, had to save his friend.

"Poor Private Franks," Biehl said.

The terrorists pulled out their six-inch blades, and went for Jimmy. Kyle's eyes burned with rage. He grabbed a gun from the soldier sitting next to him.

Aimed.

Fired.

A sharp pain stabbed Kyle in the arm. His vision blurred and the gun slipped from his fingers.

He shot his best friend.

Jimmy had always looked up to Kyle, trusted him.

And Kyle had killed him.

ANDREA TOSSED her pillow aside and grabbed a book from her nightstand. It wasn't as though she could sleep with Agent Paranoia in the next room. She considered climbing out the bedroom window and going for help but changed her mind. Her pickup had been on the fritz for a week and hiking in the dark wasn't the smartest move. Besides, in his condition the agent was as threatening as a wounded bird.

The jerk. All she'd done was try to patch him up.

"You're fooling yourself if you think he's grateful." She tossed the book aside and punched her pillow.

Something about the man troubled her. Instinct told her he wasn't bad, just hurt. She knew how animals reacted when hurt. They lashed out.

Jimmy had lashed out before she'd lost him for good. Yet lashing out was preferable to the emptiness that eventually consumed him. Emptiness caused by his secret life as a killer.

Daisy burst into frantic barks in the living room. Tying a flannel robe over her nightshirt, Andrea marched across the room and moved the chair she'd propped against the door for protection. Yeah, like in his shape the agent could hurt anybody but himself?

She flung the door open and froze at the sight of the Beta Force agent. He squeezed a pillow between his hands and gasped for breath. His head rolled from side to side as he mumbled inaudible words filled with agony.

"My God," she said.

"Help…leave no man behind, can't leave him…" he mumbled.

She went to the sofa and pried his fingers from the pillow. Running her hands across the hard planes of his chest, she searched for indication of internal damage. Nothing. She checked his wound. It festered bright red.

She grabbed the tape to finish the job, all too aware of the erratic rise and fall of his broad chest dusted with soft brown hair. She remembered the softness from before, when her fingertips had brushed against his skin. Her fingers itched at the thought.

Get a grip.

She spread ointment on the wound and adjusted the gauze in place. His eyes popped open and his glassy stare shot goose bumps across her shoulders.

"I had to do it. I didn't have any choice," he said, a panicked edge to his voice.

"Shhh. It's okay." Pulling him against her shoulder, she applied ointment to his back where she guessed the bullet had entered his body.

"I had to," he whispered into her hair.

"Hush now. You're safe." She secured the bandage.

He continued to mumble, and she wondered which killing tortured him tonight, which face haunted his dreams? These men were trained to kill and move on, to leave their consciences behind. Why did this memory haunt him?

Easing him back to the sofa, she pressed her fingertips to his forehead.

"You're burning up." She started to go in search of antibiotics but he grabbed her wrist. The grip was gentle, yet desperate.

"Help." He swallowed. "Help me." His soft brown eyes tore at her heart.

She caressed his cheek with an open palm. "I'll be right back."

He stared at her long and hard, finally loosening his

grip. He tipped his head back and closed his eyes, as if surrendering.

As she grabbed antibiotics from the cabinet, his cries of emotional pain echoed through the cabin. He ached for something that sounded like forgiveness. She went back to him, wanting to ease the pain from his voice.

She cursed her need to heal.

With a soothing touch and soft whispers, she quieted his demons. "You need to swallow this," she said, stroking the hair by his temple. "It will make you better. Open your mouth."

"No more drugs. Please…no more."

Suspecting the fever had him spinning somewhere between Mars and Jupiter, she tried a different approach.

"What's your name, soldier?"

His brows furrowed above tightly closed eyes.

"Your name, soldier, what is it?" she repeated.

"Lieutenant…Kyle…McKendrick…sir."

"Lieutenant, open your mouth. That's an order."

"No more drugs. No more," he whispered, but didn't struggle when she pried his mouth open to administer the medication.

"Swallow."

He did and she stroked his hair. "You're okay now."

"But I had to kill him. They were, they were slicing him, they were—"

"It's okay," she interrupted, not wanting to hear the gruesome details. "It's over. Let it go."

"I don't…I can't…" His voice trailed off.

Threading her fingers through his hair, she pulled him against her just as she had done for Jimmy before she'd lost him for good. She'd never forget the nights her husband had awakened screaming, staring at her as if she was a stranger. She'd held him close, desperate to squeeze away the horror. He'd cried out and whimpered, and she hadn't had a clue what demons chased him.

How could she have been so naive? She'd fought to learn his secrets and ease his pain. But he'd been sucked in too deep. It had been too late for Jimmy.

Was it too late for Kyle McKendrick?

Chapter Three

The last thing Kyle expected was to wake up with his face against a woman's breast. A beautifully shaped breast with a hardened peak, no less.

Even through the soft flannel, he knew he'd been resting on perfection. He lifted his head and blinked. How on earth did she end up here, beneath him, one hand in his hair, the other on his injured shoulder?

His good arm was buried beneath his body and his formerly numb hand rested on her hipbone. His fingers twitched.

Oscar growled.

"Shh. Let her sleep," Kyle said. *And let me enjoy the view.*

The golden retriever barked twice, warning his mistress that Kyle was awake. The woman stirred and Kyle placed his head back down. He didn't want her thinking he'd been doing anything dishonorable like fantasizing about the incredible body hidden beneath the layers of soft cotton.

As she awakened she automatically stroked his

injured shoulder to soothe him. Something wasn't right. This felt like genuine concern. She placed the back of her hand to his forehead. "Better," she whispered.

He raised his head to look at her. Her sleepy eyes widened and she nervously shifted off him.

"You're awake. I, ah, well…" Standing, she gave the belt of her robe a sharp tug. Even with her jet-black hair tousled across her shoulders, her natural beauty captivated him.

"Your fever's down," she said.

"Fever?"

"You were burning up last night. You had trouble breathing too," she explained, her gaze darting from the floor to the window, focusing on anything but Kyle.

He shouldn't be surprised. She'd been caught with her guard down, soothing the enemy. Sitting up, a sharp pain knifed between his eyes. He clutched his head with both hands.

"I'll get something for the pain," she said.

He fingered the dressing covering his wound. She didn't have to do that either. She could have let him bleed to death and called Biehl to bring the body bag.

She returned with a glass of water and pain relievers. He swallowed two pills and closed his eyes, leaning into the thick cushions of the sofa.

A warm washcloth brushed against his forehead. He opened his eyes to study her face. She focused on wiping his forehead.

"So, what, you get a bonus for keeping me alive?" he said.

She sat back and cocked her head to one side. "A bonus?"

"From Major Biehl."

"Hardly." She checked beneath his bandage. "I hate the man and everything he represents."

Sure she did.

Regardless of this woman's connection to Biehl, Kyle was still alive this morning thanks to her. He grabbed her hand, her skin soft and warm. She didn't pull away, but her fingers twitched, striking an awareness deep inside he thought he had lost years ago.

"Thanks," he said.

She smiled and he found himself wanting to touch her lips.

Whoa, Mac. You'll have to be careful with this one.

"You're almost human today," she said.

She slipped her fingers from his hand. "How about some coffee?" Without waiting for an answer she disappeared into the kitchen. He closed his eyes and listened to the sounds of *home:* pots clanging, coffee grinding and a woman murmuring to her dogs.

He had to get out of here. The drugs were making him see things that didn't exist: a caring, compassionate nurse instead of a deadly agent, a warm, inviting home when he knew the real owner must have been eliminated in order to set up shop. This was a mirage created by the clever and sadistic Major Biehl. He knew Kyle's weaknesses: the burden of guilt and ache for family, something he'd never have. The major had set the perfect trap.

Kyle would be that much smarter.

"What did you do to the real owner of this place?"

"Excuse me?" she said, pouring water into a coffee-maker.

"Never mind." She wasn't going to willingly share intel with him.

"I'll be on my way if you can spare some supplies," he called, although he knew she had no intention of letting him go. "Food and water, maybe some clothes." He ran his hands across his bare chest.

"Are you sure you can hike in your condition?"

"I have no choice. Not with Biehl so close."

"True." She padded into the living room, a frown of concern creasing her forehead.

He couldn't remember the last time someone gave a damn about what happened to him. If only her concern was genuine.

"Black?" she said, handing him a mug of coffee.

"Thanks."

She nodded and went to let the dogs out. She watched them from the window while cradling a dark green mug.

"How long have you worked for Biehl?" he asked.

She spun around and leveled him with those round, sincere eyes. "I don't work for him. I could never be involved with that..." She opened the door and one of the golden retrievers trotted inside. "My husband used to work for Biehl."

"Used to?"

"He's dead."

"Sorry."

"It's been three years. I'm over it."

She didn't sound over it.

Don't get sucked into this sad story. She was good. She almost had him believing her lies.

"I don't suppose you know if Biehl's coming back?" he said.

"He'll be back. They want my cabin to set up a base."

Which meant they could return at any moment.

The firearm taunted him from the coffee table. He leaned forward to grab it but his head pounded in protest.

"Easy now." She came up beside him. "When was the last time you ate?"

He couldn't stand her sincerity, or his body's response to her touch.

"Listen, lady," he began, trying to focus through the pain. "Stop with the games. It's your move. Either kill me or give me some supplies and let me make a run for it."

"You still think I'm with Beta Force?"

"I don't think, I know. The radio equipment, the set-up here in the mountains. Biehl knew I was coming this way. He'd been tracking me somehow. Hell, he probably set this whole thing up. That's it, isn't it? He leaked false intel to lead me directly to you. So are you going to kill me or keep me around so the major can have his fun and torture me some more?"

"I'm going to get dressed," she said, irritated. "I'll put some things together for you, including an oral antibiotic." She walked toward the bedroom, paused, but didn't turn around. "My name is Andrea. I've lived here, alone, for three years since my husband's death. I would never work for a man like Biehl."

She slammed the bedroom door.

Andrea? As in Jimmy's Andrea? No, not possible. Unless…

No, Biehl was a master to set up this agent to play the part of Jimmy's loving wife. Who better for Kyle to stumble upon but his partner's widow?

Taking a deep breath, he thanked the Almighty that he'd ended up in *Agent Andrea's* custody. Another agent would have shot him on sight, but *Andrea* took her time breaking down his defenses, convincing him that she was worthy of his trust.

Biehl had no doubt ordered her to manipulate information out of Kyle about the stolen evidence. If Kyle discovered its location he could put an end to Biehl's reign of terror. It had been Jimmy's personal mission to destroy Biehl. Yet he'd never told Kyle the whereabouts of the mysterious evidence because he didn't want to involve him in this ugly mess.

"I won't let you down, buddy," Kyle whispered, fighting back self-loathing.

One thing for sure, Kyle couldn't hang around this place and risk Agent Andrea contacting Biehl. Ignoring the pressure building behind his eyes, he went to the front hall and rummaged through the closet looking for something to bind her with so he could get away.

"Here, this might fit." She came out of the bedroom with a tan shirt dangling from her fingertips. She'd changed into tight black pants and a loose, short-sleeved shirt. Her feet were covered with leather moccasins and she'd tied her hair back, accentuating high cheekbones.

"What are you doing?" she asked.

"Don't play dumb."

She tossed the shirt at him. "Sorry, but I'm not a mind reader. You're looking for what, exactly, in my closet?"

A dog barked outside, drawing his attention to the window.

"You expecting someone?" he asked, slipping the shirt over his head. She reached out to help him. He jerked away.

"Sure. I always get visitors at seven in the morning." She went to the window and pulled aside the curtain. "It's Biehl."

Kyle froze, cursing his aching head and throbbing shoulder. He was a goner.

"He's got two men with him." She turned to him. "Hide in the attic. There's a door in the ceiling of my closet."

She'd like that, wouldn't she? An easy capture and she'd get the credit without having to exert any physical energy.

"Leaving the house might be wiser," he said.

"Whatever, you're the expert. But I don't think you'll get very far in your condition." She took a deep breath and flipped the bolt.

He raced to her side, slamming a closed fist to the door. "Don't do anything stupid. The dog likes me. I'd like to keep it that way."

Her eyes widened. "You wouldn't."

"No?"

She glanced at Daisy, who lay content under the kitchen table, then back at Kyle. She leveled him with fire in her eyes. "I should have let you bleed to death."

ANDREA FLUNG OPEN the front door, incensed at being dragged into this twisted game. She should end it right now and tell Biehl his renegade agent was hiding in her cabin.

But something held her back, and it wasn't her fear of McKendrick hurting her dog.

Staring down the stairs, she froze at the sight of one of Biehl's men pointing a rifle at Oscar.

"Oscar, come!" she called. His ears perked up but he didn't move. "Oscar, come!"

As Oscar trotted toward Andrea the soldier kept his aim steady, the barrel of the gun following her dog as he made his way up the stairs. She held her breath.

"Hello, Andrea!" Biehl called from below. "Nice to see you again."

The soldier lowered his rifle.

"What do you want?" she said. What would he do if he found out she'd aided McKendrick? She could always come clean and turn him in.

Instinct told her they'd both be killed.

"Come down here a minute," Biehl said. "I need to talk to you."

She clenched her jaw as she went down the stairs, stopping a good five feet from Biehl.

"The man we're looking for was seen in the area last night. Have you noticed anything suspicious since I was here yesterday?"

The image of a soldier crying out for absolution flashed across her thoughts.

"No. Nothing unusual." She'd keep the agent's existence a secret. Maybe she'd be able to use him as a bargaining chip: *I'll help you track your agent if you leave my family alone.*

God, she sounded cold.

"Sir, the fire's still warm." A second soldier waved his hand over the pit. Biehl shot Andrea a questioning look.

"I held a ceremony here last night," she explained. "Full moon."

"You didn't tell me you were into witchcraft." He smirked, then eyed the radio on the stairs. "Tsk, tsk. Andrea, we had an agreement. If you're not going to cooperate I'll have to take the house right now."

"Like hell you will," she let slip.

"No?" Biehl snapped his fingers and the two soldiers raced up the stairs and burst into her cabin. Oscar barked.

"Hush that mutt or I'll have my men destroy it," Biehl threatened.

"Oscar, no." She placed her hand to the dog's head to calm him. Holding her breath, she watched the men invade her home. This was it. If they found McKendrick she'd be punished or worse.

Executed.

Damn her healing obsession.

Gunshots echoed from the cabin and her heart lurched. They'd found him. Vulnerable, defenseless Kyle McKendrick, who last night had taken on a vicious mountain lion with nothing but guts and bravado, had been shot in cold blood, in her home.

Why did she care? Because she wasn't done with him, wanted answers, wanted to know how her gentle Jimmy could have been sucked into this ugly world.

"No." She started toward the house.

Biehl grabbed her upper arm. "You seem awfully upset."

"My other dog is in there."

A soldier stuck his head out the attic window and Andrea held her breath.

"I was startled by a wild animal in the attic, sir. There's nothing here but a lazy golden retriever," the soldier said. Daisy raced outside.

Andrea's body sagged with relief.

"Keep looking," Biehl ordered.

"Let go of me!" She wrenched away, but he got a hold of her elastic band and tore her hair free.

"Ah, such a beauty, wasted on someone like Jimmy."

"You really are a bastard."

He smiled and glanced at her cabin. Then, without warning, the back of his hand whipped across her cheek. She fell to the ground, dazed by the impact. Oscar barked and she heard the click of a handgun slide.

"Damn dog," Biehl swore, aiming his gun at Oscar.

"No!" She wrapped her arms around Oscar.

"Control your dog, and your mouth," he ordered. "Or I'll eliminate you both."

Fury lit his eyes. And panic. She wondered what McKendrick had on him.

"Sir?" the younger of the two soldiers questioned as he approached. "I've got something."

He handed Kyle's bloodied shirt to the major. The young soldier glanced at her with sympathy in his eyes. Apparently the young ones still had a conscience.

"What's this?" Biehl said.

"I found it near the clearing behind the house."

Biehl turned to her, narrowing his eyes. "You didn't notice anything unusual last night?"

"Nothing," she said against the buzzing in her head. Even in his darkest days Jimmy had never hit her like that.

"This man we're after, he's psychotic. It's only fair that you know," he paused, "he killed Jimmy."

Wind rushed from her lungs. No, he had to be lying to manipulate her. The bastard. Fine, she could lie and manipulate with the best of them.

"How could you let him kill one of your own men and not sentence him to death?" She stood.

Biehl eyed her. "You really didn't notice anything last night, did you?"

"You didn't answer my question." She planted her hands to her hips.

"Did you!" he shouted.

"No, I was outside by the fire," she said. "He could have gotten in through the back of the cabin."

Biehl stared off into the distance. "He's out there, in the mountains."

"My mountains," she shot back.

"Excuse me?"

"He's my husband's killer. I want him caught and punished. Like you said, I know these mountains better than anyone. I'll find him."

He smiled. "I'll do better than that. I'll send my men up there with you for protection."

Great, now what? *Buy time, girl, buy time.*

"Do they have packs with a week's worth of food and water? A change of clothes?" she challenged.

Biehl clenched his jaw. It made no sense to send these soldiers into the wild unprepared.

"Maines." He addressed the older of the two soldiers. "Stay with Andrea and," he paused, "protect her until we return with supplies."

Protect her, right. More like keep her in custody.

"We'll return in three hours with packs and two more agents." He smiled. "I'm so glad you came to your senses, for your family's sake."

So, she hadn't imagined his threat about her nephew and his family yesterday. She headed for the house, the soldier following close behind.

"Thank you for offering your home to your country," Biehl called after her.

Keep walking. Don't correct him.

She'd never agreed to let them take her cabin. But they were going to anyway. She heard the Jeep chug up the steep drive behind her.

Frustration tore at her insides, frustration at being put in this impossible situation. She'd lose her cabin. No way around it. When they returned, Biehl would bring one team to scour the mountains and another to set up a base in her cabin.

Her sanctuary.

She flung open the door. She had to get rid of her shadow soldier somehow. Then she'd run, leave it all behind.

Just like she did before.

Who are you kidding, girl?

"Nice place," the soldier said.

She glanced at him. He kept a firm grip on his machine gun.

"I like it," she said.

But not for long. Biehl would defile the tender memory of a loving husband's design of a special retreat for his wife.

It will be your sacred place, Jimmy had said with love in his eyes. Love she hadn't seen in the year before his death.

Pain burned its way up her chest.

Time to run. "I'll get my things together."

He followed her to the bedroom. She blocked the door. "Don't need any help, thanks." Oscar raced to her side and growled.

"I'll be close if you need me," he offered.

"Thanks so much." She shut the door and flopped down on the bed. Now what? Had to think, get a plan together, disappear.

She filled her backpack with clothes and strapped it on. Hesitating at the window, she remembered her most precious possession, the only thing left of her husband. She went to her dresser and pulled out Jimmy's diary, tucked it safely in her pack and went to the window. She always kept trail mix and jerky in the nylon pack in case she had to take off in a hurry.

She opened her bedroom window and helped Daisy out. Having the cabin built into the mountainside was literally a lifesaver in this situation. From her window to the ground was only four feet. She edged into the window on her belly and pushed off, landing on the hard earth.

A steady arm wrapped around her waist. Had the soldier anticipated her move?

"No." She struggled against his firm grip.

"Stop," Kyle whispered. "Why are you sneaking out?"

She turned to find him glaring down at her. Daisy stood beside him wagging her tail.

"They're going...to take the cabin," she said, her words stumbling over panic and anger. "Bringing men back to form a search party. I'm supposed to...lead them to find you."

"Biehl's coming back with reinforcements? When?"

"Three hours."

"How many?"

"Don't know."

"What else did he say?" He gripped her upper arms.

"He said you killed Jimmy."

He released her as if he'd been shocked with a thousand volts of electricity. "No, it can't be, you're not...Andy?"

The only two people who called her Andy were Jimmy and his big brother.

"I'm...yes, I'm Jimmy's wife."

Regret filled Kyle's brown eyes.

"Oh my God, he wasn't lying?" she hushed. "You killed Jimmy?"

He shook his head, but didn't speak. He took a step back and put out his hands as if to distance himself.

She turned and started to run. "Help! Out here!"

Chapter Four

Kyle couldn't move, frozen in a block of guilt.

Jimmy's wife, his beloved Andrea. And she'd seen the sin in his eyes.

Kyle had to get out of here if he stood a chance of finishing his mission. But what was left of his honor dictated that he stay and protect Andrea, give his life, if necessary, to save hers.

"He's over here!" Andrea cried.

The Beta Force soldier turned the corner. Kyle raised his hands in surrender. *Just shoot me and put me out of my misery.*

"McKendrick," the soldier said. "Inside."

Kyle marched past him, didn't look at Andrea. Couldn't look at her.

He went up the stairs and into the cabin. The soldier shoved the rifle into Kyle's ribs to encourage him to sit on the couch. Kyle sat, placed his hands to his knees. He knew the drill.

It was over. He wouldn't find the evidence, wouldn't put Biehl behind bars.

Stop acting like you've lost.

Andrea nervously shuffled through cabinets in her kitchen. He studied the beautiful woman, remembering Jimmy's stories about his high-school sweetheart who'd grown up to become a nurse. Kyle would turn green with envy at the tales of love, devotion and trust. It seemed impossible that there was a woman who nurtured as easily as she breathed, who offered complete and unconditional love.

Yet during the last year Kyle and Jimmy worked together the tales became dark and weary. Jimmy couldn't get past the realization that Biehl had used his honor to turn him into an assassin. That guilt had ripped him apart inside when his wife asked him what was wrong.

In the end, Jimmy had been the brave one. He'd stolen documentation to destroy Biehl. He didn't care about the consequences. He planned to atone for his sins by releasing everyone from Biehl's sadistic control—even if it meant sacrificing his own life.

Jimmy, why didn't you let me help you?

Kyle had had no idea what was going on until it was too late and Biehl had ordered Jimmy's death.

"You don't need me anymore. I'm out of here," Andrea announced.

Of course she was. She couldn't stand being in Kyle's presence. Good, if she fled the scene Biehl couldn't hurt her.

The soldier blocked the door. "I can't let you leave, ma'am."

"Excuse me?"

"The major will want to ask you questions about McKendrick."

"I just ran into him outside."

"You shouldn't have been outside." The soldier motioned with his gun. "Sit."

Kyle fisted his hand.

"Get out of my way, soldier," she demanded.

"I only take orders from the major, ma'am. You'll sit on the couch and wait for Major Biehl to return."

She started for the couch, a determined glint in her eye.

The soldier clicked on his radio and called in. "Major Biehl, sir? I've got McKendrick, over." No response.

"Lieutenant Maines to Major Biehl, over." He glanced out the window.

Andrea charged him from behind, shoving him out of the way and making for the door. The soldier clenched her upper arm and she struggled to wrench free.

"Take your hands off her!" Kyle shouldered the soldier in the chest, slamming him against the door. The soldier lost his grip and Andrea stumbled backwards.

Kyle ripped the gun from his enemy's hand and whacked him in the gut. The guy went down. Kyle delivered another blow to knock him unconscious and snapped cuffs from his belt to secure him.

Then he glanced at Andrea. She lay motionless on the floor beside the coffee table. "Andrea," he said, scrambling to her side.

He reached out, tentatively at first, afraid he'd make matters worse by touching her. Kyle cradled her head in one hand, while exploring her injury with the other.

The end of her coffee table had left an inch-long gash above her right temple.

Frustration tied him in knots at having caused her injury. No, she'd decided to take on the armed soldier by herself. Headstrong woman.

A woman he would protect with his life.

The sound of a whining dog drew his attention to the window. Oscar and Daisy stood on the other side, puzzling over their mistress's condition.

"Andrea?" He stroked her cheek.

She was out cold. They'd both be dead if they didn't move. He pulled her into a sitting position, hoisted her over his shoulder and opened the door.

Oscar growled at him.

"Kill me later. We've got to get your owner safe." He took the stairs carefully and picked up his pace when he hit the ground.

Keep moving, don't stop to think, breathe or look over your shoulder. Run until your legs give out. You must protect this woman.

A woman who didn't seem anything like the princess Jimmy had described. He'd told stories about his quiet and agreeable wife who'd rather eat brussel sprouts than argue with her husband.

She and Kyle had done plenty of arguing in the past ten hours.

He headed up the trail, the dogs following close behind.

Why had Biehl ordered his soldier to detain her at the cabin? To interrogate her about Kyle? Or simply to tie up loose ends by killing her too?

He spotted a cluster of spruce trees that would make

for good cover. Had to rest, catch his breath. Had to get her safe.

Pushing himself, Kyle aimed for the mass of trees, ignoring the pressure in his chest and the throbbing gunshot wound. Biehl had been a clever bastard to set up Kyle to run into Andrea. The major knew what it would do to Kyle to be saddled with his best friend's widow.

He reached cover and gently laid her down. "Andrea?"

He studied her pale skin. She looked like a fallen angel, bloodied and bruised. A part of him wanted to stroke her hair and whisper encouraging words to bring her around. She seemed so fragile and innocent.

He pulled her against his chest to remove her backpack. She smelled of earth and sunshine and life. Damned if he didn't linger a second longer than neces-sary before laying her back on the ground. He groped through the backpack, searching for a jar labeled with words any idiot could understand. He found one labeled All Heal Salve. He wiped blood from her wound with a white cotton undershirt he found in her pack, applied salve and dressed the wound.

He should have taken off into the mountains the minute Biehl showed up. Instead, he was more con-cerned with saving Andrea. He'd broken rule number one: never sacrifice your safety for another.

He stroked her face with the back of his knuckles, the same face that had worn an expression of horror when she'd realized Kyle had killed Jimmy. If only he could have explained…what?

Stop, Mac. There's no way this woman will ever accept the fact you killed the love of her life.

Putting the supplies in her backpack, he froze at the sound of a vehicle engine groaning in the distance. He glanced below and spotted Biehl's Jeep pull onto Andrea's property.

Oscar raced off.

"Get back here," Kyle whispered. The mutt ignored him and bolted toward the cabin. Defending his fortress, no doubt. Another hero, great.

It would help to know what the major was planning. Using the trees as cover, Kyle sneaked closer to listen in.

The young soldier searched the cabin while Biehl stood outside, scanning the area. He glanced in Kyle's direction. Kyle's heart raced triple time.

Get a hold of yourself. He can't see you.

The soldier came out of the cabin with the wounded soldier stumbling beside him, probably still dazed by Kyle's blow.

Kyle pulled the Glock from his waist just in case.

"He was here? And you let him escape?" Biehl screamed.

"They both jumped me, sir."

Biehl grabbed the machine gun from the other soldier and shoved the butt of the weapon into the soldier's stomach.

"Are you incompetent, lieutenant?"

The guy didn't answer.

"A wounded, drugged criminal and a weak, fragile woman jumped you?"

"They were working together, sir. I told the woman she had to stay until you returned and that's when they jumped me."

"Unacceptable!" Biehl turned to the other soldier. "Search the area. They've got to be close."

"Yes, sir."

Kyle slipped behind the tree and took a deep breath. He was one man with a hand gun against three trained murderers carrying standard-issue rifles. He went to Andrea and placed his hand to her forehead. He couldn't leave her.

The sound of a barking dog echoed across the mountains.

"Her dog! Follow it!" Biehl shouted.

Kyle couldn't believe it. Oscar was leading the soldiers away from them and up the other side of the mountain.

"Smart mutt." He ran his fingers across Andrea's cheek in a gentle caress that surprised even him. Her skin was cool and clammy.

"I don't suppose you're going to wake up for me?"

Her eyelashes fluttered.

"I didn't think so. Okay, this should be fun."

If he could get up and over the ridge they'd have adequate camouflage to head up the south side of the mountain range. He secured the gun in the waistband of his jeans, adjusted her backpack and flung her over his right shoulder. Using the strength of his legs, and ignoring other body parts that screamed in protest, Kyle marched through the rough terrain.

Shouting echoed from behind him, but he focused on the path ahead. He struggled to fill his lungs with the thin mountain air, pacing himself to get the most energy from his exhausted body. He needed time to formulate a plan to save them both from Major Biehl's next offensive.

He tried to ignore her firm, curved bottom he gripped

to keep her in place, tried to turn his face away from the tantalizing skin exposed by her jacket riding up her torso. He now had a double mission: protect Andrea and find the evidence against Biehl.

Legs on fire, Kyle trekked a good mile before spotting decent cover. He made it over the ridge and lowered Andrea to the ground. Collapsing next to her, he stared at the bright-blue sky, struggling to catch his breath.

Andrea murmured, an enchanting sound, and he traced a strand of dark hair away from her head wound. She turned to look at him and he jerked his hand away. Her green eyes did wild things to his insides.

"What...what happened?" she said.

"We're safe."

"You." She sat up and scooted away from him, terror filling her eyes.

Good, be scared as hell. That would keep things in perspective.

"You killed Jimmy."

He clenched his jaw. He didn't need to be reminded of his sin.

"The soldier led us into the cabin," she said, as if struggling to remember. "He wouldn't let me leave. He grabbed me and...you attacked him. Why?"

"He was hurting you."

"You killed my husband. Why do you care?"

"There's no time. We've got to get out of here before they find us."

She eyed the towering trees. "Where are we?"

"About a mile away from your place. I got us out of there before Biehl showed up."

"You mean, you…" She glanced in the direction of the cabin and back at him. "Carried me?"

He nodded. "That dog of yours led Biehl on a wild goose chase up the opposite side of the mountain."

She glanced at Daisy, who sat next to Kyle.

"Oscar," she hushed. "I've got to go back and find him."

"Not an option."

"But—"

"In case you haven't figured it out, Biehl's after you too. That's why the soldier wasn't going to let you leave."

"You're wrong. I'm not a part of this." She stood and wobbled.

He steadied her, pulling her close. "I didn't save your ass to have you march back down there and hand yourself over to the major."

"But I've got to find Oscar," she said.

Kyle tried a different tack: compassion. "He knows your scent. He'll find you. Now, come on. You have to lead us out of here."

"But—"

He looked into her eyes. "Please don't argue. You're on Biehl's hit list now. Maybe to get back at Jimmy or maybe because he simply enjoys killing, I don't know. But I do know we've got to get as far away as we can, as fast as we can."

She nodded. He let go of her and encouraged her to lead the way.

She hesitated, hands on her hips. "Thanks for carrying me out here."

When she glanced at him, her eyes were tinged with resentful gratitude. His heart lodged in his throat.

He didn't want her thanks, he wanted her lips on his, moist and warm, giving and wanting. He wanted to thread his fingers through her rich, dark hair and inhale its sweet scent. He wanted to—

"No," he let slip. He couldn't possibly want this woman.

"What?" she asked, a puzzled look on her face.

"I don't deserve your thanks. Let's go. What's the quickest way out of these mountains?"

She rubbed at her temples. "We'll never make it out by nightfall, but there's a remote cabin a few miles north. Not many people know about it."

ANDREA STARTED for the trail, but a wave of dizziness muddled her brain. Suddenly McKendrick was there, steadying her with an arm around her shoulder.

"Easy," he said.

Closing her eyes, she took a deep breath and willed the world to stop spinning long enough for her get away from Biehl and his men.

To get away from Jimmy's murderer, Kyle McKendrick.

Don't be a fool. He can protect you from these bastards.

She hated the thought of relying on this man. There had to be another way.

"I'm fine." She pushed away, glancing into his brown eyes, the eyes of a trained killer. Beta Force agents were soldiers without a conscience, at least that's what she'd learned after Jimmy's death.

This soldier had killed her husband. "Why?" she asked.

"Does it matter?" he said, as if he read her thoughts.

"Yes, I need to know. Was it Biehl's order?"

"Later, when we're not so close to our enemy." He walked ahead.

She started up the trail with Daisy. The dog eyed Kyle as if following his lead. But Andrea knew to keep her distance from this complicated man.

Complicated? He killed Jimmy.

Yet it was tearing him apart, she could read it in his eyes. Something didn't fit. He wasn't supposed to feel guilt and remorse. Jimmy had felt nothing during the last months of his life.

Get your hands off her! McKendrick's protest echoed in her mind.

He was protective of her. And, she'd seen regret in his eyes when she'd accused him of killing her husband. How could that be?

Her head ached, but she knew she could make it to the cabin before sunset. She wasn't so sure about McKendrick. He might act like a tough guy, but his eyes told another story. A gunshot wound didn't heal easily, especially one that he kept aggravating by doing things like attacking that soldier and carrying her up a steep trail.

He'd saved her, damn it. She didn't want to be beholden to him.

She approached Kyle and Daisy, who waited in the clearing ahead. "Need a rest?" she asked.

"I was waiting for you to catch up."

"I'm pacing myself," she said.

"All the same, I'd like you to stay close."

"Why? You planning to kill me too?"

The haunted look in his eyes shocked her, and she regretted making the quip. Then she wondered if this was some kind of absolution mission. Keep her safe to ease his guilt.

"Let's go," she said.

For hours they walked, with Daisy in between, and not a word spoken by either. She could tell the altitude was getting to him. Even a man in his excellent physical shape would be challenged by the thin air of the mountains.

Excellent shape and handsome as hell. She hadn't admitted it until now. She couldn't help but admire his body when she'd cut off his shirt. Kyle McKendrick did things to her simply by being in the same room.

She caught herself, confused by the direction of her thoughts. What was *that* about? Some kind of hostage syndrome? Was he using military mind tricks to soften her heart?

A heart that had been broken by her husband, thank you very much. She hadn't felt loved since their fourth wedding anniversary.

Following that, she'd spent two long years fighting for her husband's affections and losing miserably. Making love with Jimmy had become a physical exercise, devoid of emotion and love. She had prayed that one day the spark would return.

But it never had.

She'd died a little each time he'd refused to hold her as he'd used to when they were newlyweds. She should have known then that it was over. But she couldn't give up. True love was supposed to last a lifetime.

They stopped to eat and she noticed McKendrick's

strained expression. She shouldn't care, but the healer in her couldn't help it. Time to push back any and all compassion for the man.

"Why do you do it?" she challenged him. "What makes you kill for fun?" She realized she still wanted— no, needed—answers about her husband's mystery life.

"I did reconnaissance and rescue. People still get killed, but I wouldn't exactly call it fun."

"Then what would you call it?"

"A miscalculation. I wasn't looking for this." He motioned to his wound. "Any of it."

"What were you looking for?" She knew Jimmy had joined the military to make his father proud. She didn't understand what would compel him to join a subversive mercenary group like Beta Force.

"There are things you don't understand about the Force, about Biehl," he said.

Another few minutes passed in silence. He obviously wasn't going to continue unless pushed.

"Why were you in Biehl's hospital?" she asked. "Apparently not to treat the bullet wound."

"I had a breakdown, at least that's what they called it. I call it a case of conscience."

"Kind of late, don't you think?"

"I didn't know what the Force was until it was too late," he said. "Then I had to stick with it because I was trying to protect someone I loved."

Someone he loved? A wife? Lover? Did he treat her the way Jimmy had treated Andrea?

No, there was something different about McKendrick. A compassionate side that Biehl hadn't beaten out of him.

"What happened?" she asked.

"Biehl owned me." His gaze scanned the valley below.

Raw, emotional pain arced between them, a kind of pain Andrea recognized from living with Jimmy.

"You should have quit," she said.

"There's no quitting Beta Force."

"It's the money, isn't it?" she said, remembering Jimmy's need to buy her gifts. He was probably trying to make up for the loss of her parents who had moved two thousand miles away during her senior year of high school.

"If it was only about money…" He stared her down and she found herself edging back from the intensity of his gaze. "I tried to leave. There was an electrical fire in my parents' house. My sister barely made it out."

"I'm sorry," she whispered.

"Biehl enjoys watching the expression on your face when he describes how he'll torture someone you love."

The meaning of his words hit her like a blast of mountain air. Biehl must have threatened to harm Andrea to keep Jimmy in line, to make sure he would follow orders, no matter how heinous.

"Biehl is vicious," he said. "You should know that by now." Kyle stood and reached for the backpack. "We'd better go."

She nodded and followed him up the trail.

Jimmy had joined the Force a couple of years into their marriage, recruited by a buddy to apply to the elite team. Once Jimmy realized what it really was, why didn't he leave?

"There had to be a way out," she whispered. She

couldn't face the possibility that she'd been used as a weapon against her husband.

"No way out," Kyle grunted as he took another step.

"What about the FBI? Couldn't you go to someone like that for help?"

"Biehl is well respected in the military. Beta Force is his pet project. The higher-ups don't know much about it." His cool, dark eyes sent a shudder down her spine. "People's lives are being torn apart by this man. I need to stop him."

She eyed this wounded soldier. He wanted to end the violence, yet he'd killed…Jimmy.

Which is why you need to get away from him.

At the first opportunity she'd find a phone and warn Jimmy's brother about Biehl. Yet if this was an absolution mission for McKendrick, she doubted he'd let her go easily.

Andrea would have to outsmart the soldier to get away from him and finally escape her husband's dark past.

KYLE HIKED close enough to keep an eye on her, but not too close. Every time he looked into her eyes he heard Jimmy's voice telling one of his stories about Andrea, his high-school sweetheart.

She was different than other women. Her determination was tempered with an amazing tenderness that fascinated him. A tenderness he hadn't felt since…had he ever experienced that kind of compassion? His sister came to mind. Wendy exuded natural compassion and strength, even as she looked up at Kyle from her hospital bed. He should have seen blame or anger in her eyes. He didn't.

He continued up the trail, keeping a safe distance from Andrea. He'd been helpless to protect Wendy from the car accident that had stolen the use of her legs, but he'd make sure she'd get the expensive medical attention she needed. Joining Beta Force had been the answer and had also satisfied the reckless streak he couldn't seem to shake. He never suspected he'd be sacrificing his soul in the process.

He glanced ahead at Andrea. She was a pleasant traveling companion, not forcing conversation and giving Kyle his space.

Of course she gives you space. You killed her husband, idiot.

He spotted a cabin in the distance.

"Slow down," she said, touching his shoulder.

It was natural for her to communicate with touch. He stiffened at the contact. She glanced at him and as if suddenly realizing who she touched, she snapped her hand away.

"I want to make sure the crazy owner isn't here." She nodded toward the cabin.

"Crazy owner?"

"A writer who comes up here when he needs to fight off writer's block. The cabin's a bit primitive, but it will do. Let me check it out."

She hiked toward the cabin and his instincts flared. He shouldn't let her out of his sight. But they were far enough away from Biehl that the major couldn't hurt her.

He made for the stream and gingerly removed his

jacket. His head ached and his shoulder wound burned. He knelt down and cupped his hand, dipping it in the cool water. He needed to be alert if he was going to stay ahead of Biehl. As he splashed the frigid water against his cheek, the hair bristled on the back of his neck. The sound of a hammer cocking back echoed in his left ear. He froze.

Kyle's hands automatically went up. Biehl couldn't have tracked them.

"Don't move," a young man said. "I've got a double-barrel Winchester pointed just right to blow your head off."

A double-barrel Winchester? Not exactly standard issue.

He started to look over his shoulder but the soldier shoved the gun barrel into the side of his face.

"Don't worry about Andrea. We'll take good care of her."

Chapter Five

"Get up. Keep your hands where I can see them."

Kyle turned around, surprised to find a pimply-faced teenager staring back at him from behind the shotgun. The kid's hair was buried beneath a beat-up Stetson and the sleeves of his work shirt were rolled up above his elbows. Kyle read fear in the boy's eyes.

"We heard about you," the kid said, his voice cracking. He couldn't have been more than sixteen years old.

Digging deep for his best diplomatic skills, Kyle said, "I don't know what you heard, kid, but there are some bad guys tracking us. They plan to kill us."

"We heard you killed two kids."

Kyle's pulse raced. What grievous lies had Biehl spread about him?

"Not true," Kyle said.

"Then why are you sneaking around the Jamison place? And why did you kidnap Andrea?"

"I didn't kidnap her. We're friends."

"I don't believe you." The boy rocked from one foot to the other, adjusting his aim. "You took her against her will. We got a call from Sheriff Tate."

"Kid, listen—"

"I'm not a kid, and I know better than to take a stranger's word over the government's. Now, c'mon. Let's find Clint." The kid jerked the gun sideways.

Kyle's mind raced, ticking off his options to neutralize the punk. Murder flashed at the top of his list. He shoved it aside.

"Clint! Clint, over here!" the kid called.

A tall man in his mid-twenties appeared from a cluster of trees leading a horse. His hat hung low, shading deep-set eyes. The man was dressed like a cowboy: jeans, boots, a plaid shirt and a worn belt buckle.

"Who's this, Ricky?" the man asked, rubbing his jaw.

"Says he's Andrea's friend."

The man dropped the reins of his horse and edged closer. "A friend?"

Kyle sensed the guy's need to pick a fight.

"You gonna answer me?" Clint pushed.

Kyle glanced at the kid with the shotgun to gauge his next move. Clint shoved his rifle butt into Kyle's stomach and he fell to his knees.

"I doubt she'd be friends with a killer," Clint said.

Kyle wasn't going to be taken down by two cocky cowboys. He moaned, pretending to be hurt, waiting for his chance.

"What do we do with him?" the teenager said.

"Tie him up and call the sheriff. I'll go check on Andrea," Clint said, glancing at the cabin.

Kyle lunged, knocking him to the ground, then Kyle wrapped his arm around the guy's neck from behind.

"Stop! Get off of him!" Ricky screeched.

"Drop the weapon or I'll snap his neck."

"Let him go!" Ricky cried.

Hell, Kyle had no intention of killing the guy. But he couldn't let his kid brother know that. "I'm a trained commando," he said. "Don't think I won't snap his neck."

"Clint! Clint!" Ricky cried.

His brother struggled for air.

"Let him go, McKendrick." It was Andrea's voice.

Kyle glanced up and read the disgust on her face.

"I said, release him," she ordered.

With a jerk, Kyle removed his arm and pushed the guy off. Clint coughed, trying to get air back into his lungs.

Kyle stood, fisting his hands.

"He tried to kill Clint. He's a murderer," Ricky said.

Kyle held her gaze.

"Tie him up and bring him inside," she ordered.

Sonofabitch. She was going to turn him in to the major? She had to know her life was worth squat without Kyle's protection.

"What happened to your head?" Clint asked Andrea.

"I fell and cut it on a table."

Clint glared at Kyle.

"He didn't do this, Clint. Now come on, guys, let's go inside and talk."

Ricky continued to point the shotgun at Kyle's chest. The kid narrowed his eyes, the gun shaking in his arms. Kyle knew the feeling, the adrenaline that comes the second before you pull the trigger and kill for the first time. It was a wonder the shotgun didn't go off by accident.

Ricky licked his lips, steadied the gun and blinked. At least Kyle wouldn't have to worry about a slow, torturous death courtesy of Biehl.

"Richard," Andrea's soft voice crooned over the kid's shoulder. "Please put the gun down."

ANDREA COULD barely get the words out, panic straining her vocal chords. Ricky was young and naive, and didn't know how to handle his daddy's shotgun.

And he was aiming it at Kyle. She needed him alive. He could be her bargaining chip with Biehl, and she still needed answers to help her understand how she'd lost Jimmy.

You lost him because you failed to save him.

Guilt burned her eyes.

"Look what he did to Clint." Ricky's arms shook.

Andrea's heart pounded in her chest. The fact was, McKendrick *could* have killed Clint, but he'd chosen not to. The man was a puzzle of contradictions.

"Richard. Please give me the gun," she coaxed. "I don't want anybody to get hurt."

"Army guys came to the farm and they said this guy killed two kids."

She read the anger in McKendrick's eyes. He didn't appreciate being labeled a child killer.

"Those men aren't who they say they are," she explained. "They're after me, too. Please, put the gun down so we can go inside and talk."

"We found Oscar. He brought us here. Me and Clint," the boy rambled.

She sensed Clint's ego was bruised by Kyle's defensive move. She hadn't realized they had visitors until she'd seen Kyle's arms go up. Her belly had tied into knots, thinking it was Biehl's men.

The Simpson boys didn't understand the situation. And she did?

She could have the boys call Biehl and turn in McKendrick, but she didn't want to involve them and put their lives at risk.

"Thank you for finding Oscar for me, Richard. Now, please, give me the shotgun."

"No! I've got to protect you from this killer."

"He won't hurt us. He actually saved my life. Twice."

She glanced into McKendrick's eyes and held his gaze. *Why did you have to help me when I want desperately to hate you? Blame you?*

Blame? *Look in the mirror, girl.*

"I don't trust him," Ricky said.

"I won't let you become a murderer on my behalf. Clint, tie up Mr. McKendrick and bring him inside. I'll explain everything."

She reached around and placed a hand over Ricky's. His fingers loosened a bit. "That's it, give me the gun."

He jerked the gun away, closed one eye and aimed at Kyle.

"Don't do this." She was afraid to look at Kyle, afraid to see the look of panic just before death.

She realized she didn't want him to die.

She was more than a little mixed up.

"Clint needs to tie him up first," Ricky said.

Clint grabbed a leather strap from his saddle. With a cocky smirk he bound Kyle's hands behind his back.

Clint gave the bindings a final, sharp tug and Kyle's jaw twitched.

She read frustration in his eyes, and something else: the burn of helplessness. She'd felt that burn after months of trying to heal her husband.

When she'd realized she couldn't.

"It's okay, now, give me the gun," she said.

He begrudgingly gave it up.

"We're all okay now. Let's go inside."

KYLE WAS anything but okay with his wrists bound tight and his temper dangerously close to the boiling point. She pulled the gun from the kid's trembling hands and glanced at Kyle, her eyes filled with sympathy.

No, not possible. He was hallucinating again.

She started for the cabin, holding onto the teenager's arm, probably to make sure he didn't change his mind and shoot Kyle in the chest. Oscar barked and wagged his tail, happy to be reunited with his mistress.

"Get moving." Clint jabbed Kyle in the back with the barrel of his gun.

Captured. Again. That burn started deep in the pit of his stomach and snaked its way up to his chest. He'd only been captured a couple of times, but each time had left its mark on his psyche. He relived the torture when he closed his eyes at night—pain, fear, helplessness. He could ignore the pain and control the fear, but the helplessness tore through him like the claws of a grizzly.

Another poke in the side nearly made him spin around and deliver a head butt to his captor. A growling dog stopped him. He glanced at Daisy, who was baring her teeth at Clint.

"What's the problem, Daisy?" Clint reached over to pet the dog. She snapped and Clint jerked his hand away. "What the hell?"

Kyle almost smiled. The damned dog was protecting him.

Andrea glanced over her shoulder. "Clint, stop playing with the dog and come inside."

Daisy rubbed against Kyle's leg, wagging her tail. Clint shot him a dirty look.

He gave the bindings a subtle tug. Houdini couldn't escape from Clint's expert knot. He glared at the open door to the cabin. Was it Andrea's plan to hold him and contact Biehl? No, she knew not to get into bed with that bastard.

What, then? Turn him over to the local authorities for killing her husband?

Hell, if she'd wanted revenge she could have let the kid blow him to bits. It would have been faster and easier than having to explain her husband's involvement in Beta. But Kyle suspected she didn't want to ruin the teenager's life by making him a killer.

Damn, what was she up to?

He hoped she wasn't counting on these bozos to protect her. They hadn't a clue how to keep somebody safe from a man like Biehl. If Andrea wanted to live, Kyle was her only chance.

He went to the cabin, trying to look as nonchalant as possible with his hands tied behind his back. He struggled against his bindings, the leather cutting into his skin with each twist. The one-room cabin was cozy, with a double bed, a kitchen table and a couple of chairs facing the fireplace. A desk and typewriter sat in the corner, and above the desk hung a bulletin board with charts and photographs. There was no glass in the windows, only screens and shutters to close out the world.

He sat at the kitchen table, hoping she wasn't planning to serve her guests anything to eat. What would Miss Brilliant do then? Feed him?

"What's really going on?" Clint asked. "Sheriff Tate stopped by with some military guy and said a crazed soldier was out there killing kids."

Andrea lit the woodstove and put on water. She acted the perfect hostess, as comfortable in the kitchen as she was climbing mountains.

"That military guy was probably Major Biehl. He's the bad guy. Trust me." She placed tea bags in two mugs.

"How did you come to be with him?" Clint nodded at Kyle.

"We're both running from Biehl." She turned, leaned against the counter and crossed her arms over her chest.

She glanced at Kyle and he knew he was a goner. This was it. She'd tell these boys that Kyle had killed her husband and they'd beat the crap out of him first, then turn him over to the authorities.

"Biehl had my husband killed," she said.

Kyle nearly choked. What the hell?

"Had him killed?" Clint questioned.

"Biehl is a bastard, Clint. His private army has taken over my cabin. I'm homeless and on the run."

"You can stay at the farm," Ricky offered.

She glanced at Kyle. He read her thoughts: *If you care about someone, you protect him.*

"It's best if I keep moving." She sat across the table from Ricky. "My husband worked for Biehl and did terrible things. Biehl had him killed and now I'm on the hit list. Kyle might be the only one who can help me."

"No!" Clint jumped to his feet, nearly knocking the table over. "I won't believe that this…this jerk can help you. He's evil. I can see it in his eyes."

Of course he could. Anger, hatred, death. It was all there.

"I'm getting Sheriff Tate," Clint said.

Kyle pulled against his bindings. If they handed him over to the locals, Andrea would never survive. Couldn't let that happen, couldn't let Biehl hurt her.

"Clint, sit down," she said.

The man sat in his chair and crossed his arms over his chest. Ricky looked from Clint to Andrea and back to Clint.

"I know you're trying to protect me and I appreciate that," she said. "But right now the best thing you can do is let me handle this. My way."

Kyle glanced at her and wondered what she planned to do.

"My husband's family thinks he died a hero," she started. "I want them to continue thinking that way. I need a little time to figure out how to make Major Biehl get what he deserves, without ruining Jimmy's memory. Can you understand that?"

Clint nodded, but wouldn't look at her.

She glanced at Kyle. That determined expression shot panic through him.

"I need to work through this on my own," she said, looking at Clint. "It could mean my life and another person's life, someone I care about very much."

Who the hell was she talking about?

"Not this creep! Don't tell me you've got feelings for him." Clint accused.

"No, I don't have feelings for McKendrick," she said.

He clenched his jaw. The bindings were cutting off his circulation.

"The truth is, I need McKendrick's help or this person I care about could be hurt. I can't let that happen. Do you understand?"

"I guess."

"Please help me by keeping our whereabouts a secret. Don't tell anyone you've seen us. Can you do that?"

"Pa's responsible for this place when the owner isn't here. I'll have to tell him what's going on."

"I understand. But no one else."

Clint narrowed his eyes. "You sure you know what you're doing?"

"Absolutely." She stood and grabbed the pot of hot water. She reached over and filled two mugs.

"I'll respect your wishes, but I don't trust him," Clint said. "You should keep him tied up so he can't hurt you."

"Exactly what I plan to do," she said with a smile.

Kyle seethed. She wouldn't.

Clint and Ricky drank tea in silence. "You sure we shouldn't call the sheriff's office?" Clint offered.

"No, really. I'd prefer you stay out of this."

Clint pushed away from the table and stood. "If Sheriff Tate stops by the farm and asks outright, I can't lie to him."

"I wouldn't expect you to," she said.

"What if the military man stops by again?" Clint asked.

"You don't want Biehl to know you came into contact with us," Kyle offered. "It could put you in danger."

"Danger, my ass," he shot back, puffing out his chest.

She went to Clint and touched his arm. "McKendrick's right. Don't tell anyone but your dad. I wouldn't want anything to happen to you guys."

Clint stood tall. Ricky glanced at his feet in embarrassment. She had them completely under her spell.

Clint nodded and headed for the door, Ricky close on his heels. Clint turned and pointed a finger at Kyle. "You lay a hand on her and you're a dead man as sure as I'm standing here."

Kyle kept his mouth shut. He knew the bravado was meant to impress Andrea. The door closed behind them and she let out a sigh.

"Nice work, now untie me," Kyle ordered.

"Not yet." She flipped a kitchen chair backwards and straddled it. She stared him down, the rise and fall of her chest making his pulse quicken. His body instinctively reacted to the beauty that sat only inches away.

No, his pulse raced because he couldn't stand feeling powerless.

"Maybe I feel safer this way," she said.

"You know I wouldn't hurt you."

"Do I?"

"You told those guys you needed my help. It sounded like you trusted me to protect you."

"I was lying. I don't want them getting involved in this. I need to protect my family. How do I make that happen?"

He read determination in her eyes. And love.

"What family?"

"Jimmy's brother and his children. Biehl threatened to hurt my nephew."

"Unless?"

"I found you."

"And you have. You could turn me over to him."

She leaned back in the chair. "You're serious. See, that's what I don't get. You're Beta Force, yet you put my safety before your own. You could have killed Clint, but you didn't. What's your deal, McKendrick?"

"My name is Kyle." He didn't like her calling him by his last name.

"What are you after?" she pushed.

"The evidence Jimmy was going to use to put Biehl away." He paused. "If it even exists."

"Why did you kill my husband?"

He glanced at the floor. "You don't want to hear this."

She slapped his cheek. Not hard, but hard enough to get his attention.

"Why?" she demanded.

He stared into her eyes. His penance was not only having to protect her, but having to confess his sin as well. "Biehl left him behind. He wouldn't land the chopper to rescue him. Jimmy was being tortured by the enemy. I…"

She gripped his shoulders. "You what?"

He glared at her. "I couldn't let him die like that. He was my friend, so I shot him."

"Why should I believe you?"

He swallowed back the burn of verbalizing his sin. "You shouldn't. Don't believe me, or anyone from Beta." He studied her dark-green eyes and wondered what she was thinking, what she'd do next. If she were smart she'd negotiate with Biehl: her freedom for renegade agent Kyle McKendrick. But then, Kyle feared that revenge drove Biehl to destroy everyone connected to Jimmy. Including Andrea.

"Whatever," she said, defeat in her voice. "After tonight I'll be rid of you."

"Meaning what?"

"Tomorrow morning I'm off to contact my brother-in-law and warn him about Biehl. Alone."

"I need to protect you."

"No, you really don't. I want everything relating to Beta Force out of my life. For good this time."

"You can't defend yourself against these men."

"I won't have to. They'll never find me."

With a sigh, she stood. She had no intention of untying him, and planned to go off on her own?

No, he owed it to Jimmy to make sure she was okay. He had to get this situation under control.

She went to the bed and dug something out of her backpack. When she turned, he sprang to his feet and charged, flattening her to the mattress.

It was a good thing Oscar and Daisy were outside. He hated to think which part of his appendage would be bleeding if Oscar saw his attack.

"Untie me," he demanded, his face nearly touching hers.

"Get off!"

She squirmed to get out from under him, but she was no match for his hundred-and-eighty-pound frame.

"I'll get off when you untie me," he said. "Go on, reach around and do it."

Instead, she pushed at his shoulders with flattened palms. A brief image of this woman in the throes of a wild sexual encounter crossed his thoughts: black hair flying about her face, wild eyes, honey-sweet lips slightly parted.

"Now what? Are you going to rape the wife of the man you killed?" She glared. "I know about you, soldier. How you killed and raped and destroyed for Beta Force. If I let you go, you're going to try and destroy me!"

Destroy her? Yeah, he could see why she'd think that. He'd pretty much destroyed everything else in life. The image of his sister being cut from the car wreckage raced across his thoughts.

He slid off of her and sat on the floor beside the bed. "I'm sorry. I didn't mean to hurt you."

ANDREA FROZE at the sound of his voice. He was either a good actor or...

Or Kyle McKendrick was truly sorry. He wasn't a ruthless killer like her husband. Kyle felt things: regret, shame and guilt.

It didn't matter. She needed to get away from him.

She sat up and went to the kitchen. She couldn't

bring herself to untie him, not yet. She glanced over her shoulder and noticed blood seeping through his shirt.

"Sit at the table," she said.

"Why?" He didn't move.

"Your wound is festering. I can at least fix that before we part ways."

He straightened and did as ordered. She'd have to untie him to tend his wound.

She went to him and hesitated as she reached for the leather strap.

"I won't hurt you, Andrea. You know that," he said.

She hated that she believed him.

She loosened his bindings and noticed his wrists were raw, probably because Clint had bound them too tight. She'd have to put ointment on his skin.

"Take off your shirt," she said, walking to the kitchen to heat more water. She shouldn't be helping this man.

Yet once she tended his injuries, they were even. The thought of spending any more time alone with Kyle did wild things to her insides. It wasn't fear that set her on edge. She recognized a tenderness in him that belied his violent nature. On the other hand, she was emotional and confused.

And she found herself attracted to her husband's killer.

She shook her head to clear it of runaway hormones. If she ever fell for a man again, it would not be a man like Kyle McKendrick.

She focused on contacting Jimmy's brother and explaining the danger. How was she going to do that? Call and say, "Hey, Tom, sorry I abandoned the family three years ago. I'm calling to warn you that the murderers your baby brother hung around with are coming after your son?" Somehow she didn't think Tom would believe her.

"Andrea!"

She jumped at the sound of Kyle's voice and turned. He had stripped to the waist. She ground her teeth.

"I said your name three times," he said. "Should I take the bandage off?"

"No, I'll do it." She turned back to the sink and closed her eyes, struggling to erase the image of his broad chest, sleek and strong, covered with soft, brown curls. She remembered the feel of his chest from when she'd cut off his shirt last night.

"Not good," she whispered.

She found it difficult to concentrate on warming water with Kyle McKendrick in the same room. *That's because he killed your husband.*

More like she found herself attracted to a bad boy. Or was it that she wanted to heal him, succeed in saving him because she'd so pitifully failed to save Jimmy?

She dug a jar of salve from her pack and spread the ointment on a washcloth she'd dipped in the water. Taking a deep breath, she went to Kyle. She didn't want to make eye contact and she sure as heck didn't want to ogle his chest. She glanced out the window at the open country and handed him the medicinal cloth. "Here, hold this while I remove the bandage."

She peeled the tape from his skin. His head tipped back and he closed his eyes.

"I'm sorry. Does it hurt?" she said.

"No. You're fine."

Ha, she was anything but fine. Every time she touched this man her brain short-circuited.

Her husband's killer.

Her personal protector.

A murderer.

Her savior.

Enough!

She fingered the bandage and pulled it away from his skin. He didn't move. She took the cloth from his hand and placed it to the wound, bracing her other hand on her hip to prevent it from landing somewhere it shouldn't.

Her gaze drifted to Kyle's face. His jaw twitched, the only sign he felt discomfort from the compress. She nearly reached out to stroke his hair, to whisper comforting words, but she caught herself. It was natural to want to comfort an injured man. Comforting this man was neither natural nor right.

Removing the cloth, she put clean gauze in place and re-bandaged the wound. She glanced at his face. He hadn't moved, and for a minute she thought he might have drifted off.

"I'm done," she said.

He opened his regretful, yet appreciative brown eyes. She went to the sink and rinsed the washcloth.

"He talked about you all the time," he said.

She turned to face him. "What?"

"Jimmy. I could tell by the tone of his voice how much he loved you."

"This is some kind of manipulation, right? Mind games or something?"

"No, Jimmy and I were good friends and partners."

"My God. McKendrick? You're his friend, Mac?"

Mac was the mysterious "friend" who had recruited Jimmy into joining Beta Force. She turned away from him, nausea rising in her chest.

After Jimmy's death, her pain had been tempered by blaming everything on his elusive "friend," the man who had lured him into joining. Jimmy wasn't bad, she'd told herself for months after his death. It was his friend, Mac, who was the bad influence. He'd convinced Jimmy to do horrible things, including lying to Andrea.

Only, the "friend" wasn't around when Andrea and Jimmy fought, when Jimmy careened over the edge and crushed her hope of things ever being right again.

"He mentioned you." She ambled across the room and placed the ointment on the mantel above the cold fireplace.

For years after Jimmy's death, she had wished his mysterious friend dead, hoped and prayed that he'd be shot down and killed during some meaningless mission. Instead, not only had McKendrick killed Jimmy, but he'd taken advantage of her nurturing nature. She'd cared for, maybe even saved the life of, the one man who was responsible for her life going to hell.

And yet, McKendrick wasn't done. What did he really want? To bed Jimmy's wife for sport? Wouldn't that be rich? Destroy the man, then destroy the woman he loved?

Three years of repressed emotion consumed her. She struggled to breathe as she gripped the wooden mantel. Glancing across the room, she noticed the rifle Stephen Jamison kept beside his desk in case an unwelcome mountain animal paid him a visit. She went to the desk and shuffled papers.

"What are you doing?" he asked.

"Looking for something."

Vengeance. Justice. Peace.

She grabbed the rifle, spun around and aimed it at Kyle. "You killed him and now you're out to destroy me too?"

"Put the gun down." He raised his hands.

"You dragged him into this and now, what do you want?"

"I don't want anything. Not from you."

"I don't believe you. Outside," she ordered.

She wouldn't mess up Jamison's cabin with this murderer's blood.

Guilt burned its way up her chest. McKendrick wasn't solely to blame for Jimmy's fate. Andrea could have saved him, should have saved him.

Her hands shook and her eyes burned. She stared down the gun barrel at Kyle, suddenly confused by earlier feelings of compassion and tenderness.

This man…this horrible man. She wanted him dead. It would satisfy Biehl, satisfy her need for justice.

He went outside.

"Sit," she ordered the dogs, so they wouldn't get in the way.

"Jimmy was a trusting kid," she accused, shutting the door. She aimed the gun at McKendrick's naked back. "You lured him into hell!"

"No, I cared about him." He turned to face her. "We were partners."

"So were we, you bastard." She pulled the trigger.

Chapter Six

Kyle's heart slammed against his chest. It wasn't that she was a bad aim. Hell, a kid could have nailed him at this range. She'd missed on purpose.

"Stay away from me!" she cried, marching back to the cabin.

He grabbed her arm. "Wait a second."

She wrenched free from his grasp. "Don't touch me."

"Jimmy was a big boy. He made his own decisions."

"He trusted you. I spent months trying to figure out how I'd lost him. I lost him to you and Biehl and the rush of violence. To think I tended your gunshot wound." She paused. "I cared for you."

He followed her into the cabin, trying to ignore the anguish in her eyes. He had to shove aside the guilt eating away his insides and treat this woman like a hostage needing to be rescued. It was the only way he could survive her presence and help her escape Biehl.

The dogs pranced around her legs and she ordered them outside. When she reached for her backpack, he came up behind her and closed his fingers gently around her wrist. The lightning in her eyes sent a clear message: Kyle was her enemy.

"We have to come to an agreement," he said. "Please, sit down."

A strange expression crossed her features. God, he wished he could interpret it. It would be helpful to know what she was feeling, other than hatred.

She ambled to the chair in front of the cold fireplace. Panic shot through his body. He hadn't a clue what to say.

He slipped on his shirt and faced her. "I can imagine how you must be feeling."

She glared at him.

"Okay, maybe I can't." He said.

Her gaze dropped to her hands, balled in her lap.

"Biehl won't give up until he finds you," he said. "I'm not going to let that happen. Nothing else matters."

"What does he want with me?"

She looked at him and his heart caught. He wanted to take her in his arms and assure her that everything was going to be okay. He knew she'd recoil at his touch.

"It's the evidence Jimmy had on him. Biehl might think you know where it is."

"I didn't know Jimmy was a mercenary but I'm supposed to know about damning evidence?" She shook her head. "Seven years of marriage and I didn't know my own husband."

Taking a deep breath, he pushed aside the ache in his chest. He knew how much Jimmy had loved her. He'd been devoted to Andrea until Beta Force turned him into a cold-blooded killer. That's what she remembered now: the angry, violent Jimmy Franks. Kyle could see it in her eyes.

"I'm going to get you away from Biehl," he said.

"I don't need your help." Her gaze snapped up to challenge his. "I need to get to my brother-in-law and warn him."

"Not wise. Biehl probably has his house under surveillance."

She leaned her head against the oak rocker and closed her eyes.

"I'm sorry you got dragged into this," he said. Where had that come from? He'd dismissed sentimentality years ago. "My goal is to keep you safe. In the meantime, if you can think of anyplace Jimmy might have hidden the evidence—"

"Oh no, don't get me involved." She stood and paced to the window. "I'm going to warn my family and disappear where no one can find me."

"But you might be able to help."

She turned to him. "I don't care about your crusade. The government knows what Biehl is and they do nothing. They let him lead those suicide missions, and the dead soldiers get their honorary burials and everyone's happy."

"Everyone?"

She went to the bed and pulled a piece of government stationery from her backpack. "This is what's left of Jimmy. His honor. His family believes he died an honorable soldier. If they ever found out what he really did it would break their hearts."

"More people will die if Biehl isn't stopped."

She ran her finger across the worn folds of the letter. "He can't be stopped. The government doesn't care.

You'll expose Biehl, and the men who died under his command, the ones who died with honor...all those families will be haunted by the possibility that their husbands, fathers and brothers killed innocent people."

"We can help the soldiers who are being blackmailed by Biehl. It's what Jimmy wanted."

"Jimmy's gone." Her gaze shot up to challenge his. "I wish you were with him."

Her words burned worse than his wound. She despised him. Kyle represented death and destruction.

"What's in this for you, anyway?" she said. "You hope to get your honor back, is that it?"

"This isn't about me," he said. "It's about families who are threatened by Biehl, the children. Surely you care about children?"

Her eyes shot up to challenge his, but the anger dissolved into something sad and anguished. "I love children."

"Then consider the kids whose fathers have to kill because they value their children's lives."

A spark flashed in her eyes, then she refocused on the cold fireplace. She'd shut him out, at least for now.

"The sun's going down," he said. "I'll get wood for the fire."

"You do that."

He studied the beautiful face of a woman who looked as if she'd lost her best friend. More like been saddled with her worst enemy. But he wasn't the enemy, not the way she thought. Kyle wanted to protect her, to right the wrong. Nothing could erase his sin, but he could keep her safe. Taking a deep breath he walked to the door.

"Could you let the dogs in?" she asked, not looking at him.

"Sure."

He opened the cabin door and whistled for the dogs. They came running and he closed the door behind him.

Kyle spotted an ax wedged in a thick piece of tree trunk and headed for it. Not a good idea unless he wanted to rip open his shoulder wound.

He knew damn well it would be torture for Andrea if he did. Her healing nature would compel her to tend his wound. Yet touching him would make her sick.

He decided to sit down on a tree stump and give her some space.

Jimmy's wife. Kyle had a hard enough time sleeping at night without having to sleep in the same room with the woman he'd widowed.

He recalled Jimmy's erratic and violent behavior during the last year of his life. Kyle had suggested he separate from his wife because Kyle wasn't sure Jimmy could control his anger around his beloved Andy.

From what Jimmy had said, Andrea fought to save their marriage. She'd push Jimmy until he was up against the wall. Kyle knew that the more you pushed someone the faster they ran, until suddenly they disappeared right before your eyes. Kyle had pushed Jimmy, but when Jimmy started to slip away, Kyle had let up. He didn't want to lose him completely, not like he'd lost his sister. Not like he was about to lose Andrea.

Hell, this woman isn't yours to lose.

She'd never offered anything beyond medical care to a stranger. Yet before, when she was pinned beneath him on the bed, he could have sworn he read desire in her eyes.

Ridiculous.

Andrea had been incensed when she'd found out Kyle was the bastard who'd introduced Jimmy to the Force. Kyle doubted she'd listen to his explanation about how he, too, had been duped by Biehl. If it hadn't been for Kyle's ignorance about Biehl's true motivations, Jimmy might still be alive.

Guilt gnawed at his insides the way it had each day for the past three years. He couldn't change what had happened to Jimmy, but Andrea…he had to get her away from here.

He'd make sure she was safe and he'd be on his way, alone, as always. A familiar emptiness settled low. To think he'd actually grown used to her presence.

Grabbing a couple of thick pieces of wood and some smaller sticks for kindling, he went to the cabin. It was quiet as he approached. Out of courtesy he knocked before entering.

No answer.

"Andrea?" He pushed open the door.

She was gone.

TAKING OFF was her only option. She couldn't stand to be around McKendrick. She couldn't stand her conflicted feelings.

She hated him, wanted him dead. Yet there was something about McKendrick that reached out to her, tapping into her compassion.

Which is why she had to run.

She was good at running, from her enemies, from her friends.

From the truth.

How long could she keep blaming others for her own failure? She'd encouraged Jimmy to join the military; she didn't protest when he wanted to join Beta Force.

Yet she'd been unable to guide him out of his hell. Her failure.

Which made her even more determined to protect her brother-in-law's family. It had taken hours, and the sun had gone down, but she finally found a trail leading to the two-lane highway that cut through the mountains. She cautiously approached the highway rest stop. With the dogs at either side, she peeked her head up to see if it was safe. There was only one car, parked at the far side of lot from the public phone. She pulled off her backpack and dug inside for her notebook. Her hands touched Jimmy's diary.

Would she ever be strong enough to read it?

"Can't think about that now," she whispered. She noticed Daisy eye the valley below, as if waiting for McKendrick to join them.

Andrea felt relieved to be rid of him, even though instinct told her he wouldn't physically hurt her. Curse her instinct.

She found her brother-in-law's phone number, ordered the dogs to stay back, and went to the pay phone. Her fingers trembled as she punched the buttons. What was she going to say?

The phone rang once, twice, three times.

The answering machine picked up. "You've reached

the Franks's house. We're busy making pie," a little girl said. "Leave your phone number and my mom will call you back."

Andrea closed her eyes. She'd only seen her niece once, when she was three. She had to be almost six. She sounded so grown up.

Squeezing the receiver, she hung up the phone with a sigh. This was not something she could explain on an answering machine.

She scrambled back to the trail, frustrated at being unable to warn her brother-in-law about the danger. What now? Hitch a ride into Colorado Springs and talk to him in person?

"What do I do, Jimmy?"

If only he were here to give her advice.

She'd always relied on his good sense and judgment. At least until the last year of his life. She pulled Jimmy's diary from her backpack. Brushing her hands across the cool, soft leather, she opened to the first page. The full moon illuminated the diary and she read the entry, *A New Assignment.*

He wrote about Beta Force, Mac and the hostages they'd saved. She sensed the pride in his words, the excitement.

She flipped through the pages and her eyes caught on the words, *I've lost her for good.*

Her heart skipped as she continued to read on.

I can see it in her eyes. My self-loathing has turned me into a monster. Mac says I need help, that I'm not thinking straight. But I know exactly what to do. MB has taken everything from me: my honor, my self-respect, Andrea. Now I will take it all from him. I will destroy him if it kills me.

And it did.

She closed the book. "No more," she whispered.

It hurt too much. She had to solve this current challenge on her own, without looking to Jimmy or anyone else for help.

It would be silly to leave a safe spot where she had access to a working phone. She'd call her brother-in-law back in an hour, and then every hour after that until she reached him.

The sound of a truck kicking into gear drew her attention to the road. Peeking over the top, she noticed high, bright headlights pierce through the darkness. Army trucks. Two of them pulled into the lot and half a dozen men climbed out.

Oscar barked, but luckily the sound was drowned out by truck engines.

"Move," she ordered the dogs. She raced in the opposite direction, following the trail that paralleled the highway.

Beta Force seemed to be everywhere, but she had to reach Tom. Had to warn him.

Tom had uprooted his family and taken a job near his little brother to be close. Even after Jimmy had died, Tom had stuck around, hoping that Andrea would come back to the family.

Her secret prevented her from returning. It would tear her apart to look into Tommy's eyes and lie about how much she missed Jimmy.

Male voices sounded from above. Andrea couldn't get far enough away from Biehl. Taking a deep breath, she chose a trail that led into the heart of the mountains. She'd hide there until they were gone.

She drifted deeper into the woods, the moon illuminating her path. The stillness of the night used to give her comfort. Tonight she imagined soldiers behind every tree, guns drawn and ready to fire.

Solitude had been her companion for the last three years. She'd enjoyed so many wonderful nights meditating beside the fire and curling up on her sofa. Her life had finally gained a stability she thought never to have again.

Then Biehl had blasted her serenity to pieces.

Followed by McKendrick.

I couldn't let him die like that.

His confession haunted her. According to Jimmy's diary, McKendrick had encouraged him to get help.

Was it really fair to link McKendrick with Biehl?

Maybe not, but it was wrong that her heart raced whenever McKendrick got too close.

Sure, she'd met other men in town on her weekly visit to the grocery store. A few had even asked her out. She'd turned them down, saying it was too soon after her husband's death. In reality, she'd disconnected emotionally from Jimmy long before he'd died. She just couldn't bring herself to trust another man.

Oscar hesitated then growled. Daisy's ears pricked and she sat in a perfect dog sit next to Andrea.

"What is it, boy?" Andrea asked, kneeling down and stroking Oscar's thick coat. He growled again, a low rumble from deep in his chest. Walkie-talkies chattered from the valley below. More Beta Force agents. She spied the glow of a campfire.

"We've got to get out of here." In a panic, she abruptly turned and lost her balance, sliding toward the sound of radio communication. She flung her arms out to grab something to stop the momentum.

What would they do when she so conveniently dropped into their laps? Have a little fun before they turned her over to Biehl?

She flailed her arms, horrified at the thought of the thugs capturing her. With a jerk, she came to a sudden stop. Her backpack had caught on something. She swallowed a gasp of relief, afraid that they'd hear even her slightest breath. All they had to do was shine a flashlight up the mountainside and they'd see her dangling there like a ripe apple ready to be plucked.

With a calming breath she looked to either side and above, where the dogs paced. If she broke free, she'd careen into their camp.

Oscar, frustrated at his mistress's predicament, barked.

"Hush," she ordered.

She dangled, helpless like a duck in a carnival game, waiting to be picked off by a kid. Or did Biehl want her alive for his own, sick purpose?

Enough. She pushed aside the gruesome possibilities.

Afraid to chance her backpack's precarious hold, she looked for something to grab on to. She spotted a sturdy branch and, biting her lower lip, reached for it with her left hand.

"Are you sure, private?" a man asked from below. "Could have been a wolf."

"It was definitely a domestic animal."

"Go ahead and check it out. Take Dilling with you."

"Yes, sir."

Panic watered her eyes. They were coming for her.

In a desperate move, she stretched a little farther, her body twisting, straining against the solid earth. She closed her fingers around the branch and her backpack gave way. A stifled scream escaped her lips. She whipped her right hand around to clasp the branch as a shower of small rocks tumbled down the mountainside. She prayed that one of them didn't hit a soldier between the eyes.

"What was that?" a soldier said.

She scrambled for leverage, edging her way up the mountain. She could do this. She could save herself.

A soft crack echoed from the ridge above and she froze. How had the soldiers managed to get there so fast?

Her pulse raced into her throat as she clung tighter to the branch. Any minute now she fully expected to be staring down the barrel of a gun.

"Grab my hand," a male voice whispered.

McKendrick. She looked into his deep-brown eyes. He extended his steady hand, but fear paralyzed her.

"I figure you've got ten seconds before they find you," he said. "It's either me or them."

Shocked back to reality, she slapped her palm against his wrist and pushed with her feet. In one swift motion he pulled her to the ridge beside him. Her body trembled with adrenaline and fear.

"Shh. You're okay," he said. "Take a deep breath. Concentrate on my voice."

He held her close and she found comfort in his arms. She shouldn't, damn it. Yet she felt protected and safe.

And confused. He'd rescued her. Again.

She glanced into his eyes. "Thanks."

KYLE'S HEART skipped a beat. She felt perfect against him, so soft and warm.

Shake it off, McKendrick. She's grateful that you saved her ass, that's all.

"See that boulder over there?" He pointed. "We need to hide behind it until they lose interest."

She stared at him with those big green eyes. He wanted to kiss her senseless. Instead he coaxed her away from the edge.

"Tell the dogs to stay up on the ridge."

She gave the dogs a hand signal and they sat, waiting. She and Kyle slipped between a few pine trees to make their way to the boulder.

She slid her hand into his and he lit on fire. The thought of her reaching for him was tearing him apart. They found safety behind the boulder and he shielded her from their enemies.

"Stay behind me," he said. He knew the drill. If the soldiers heard the slightest sound they'd order a full search of the area.

He wouldn't let Andrea know that, not with her nerves stretched taut. His job was to keep her calm so he could get her safely out of here.

He put his arm around her.

"How did you find me?" she whispered.

"No matter where you go, I'll be right behind you until I know you're safe."

She turned into his chest and clutched his shirt. "I called Jimmy's brother but no one was home."

"Shhh."

"I have to warn them," she said, desperation edging her voice.

He stroked her hair. "You can't do that if you're caught. Now relax."

A couple of minutes passed, her body molding against his as though they were made for each other. If he wasn't about to get his brains blown out, he'd be tempted to turn his face a few inches and—

This is Jimmy's wife! No matter how stunning her eyes or how soft her hair, he couldn't kiss her, not the way he wanted to kiss her. Not even if she demanded it. Now *there* was an insane image: Andrea demanding a kiss.

"Listen," he whispered. "If something happens to me, you get the hell out of here. Got it?"

"But—"

"No argument. Stay out of sight until you know it's safe. Then run."

Her hand edged its way into his palm, delicate, gentle fingers, fingers of a healer who didn't deserve to be hunted and stalked like a wild animal.

He closed his eyes. She shouldn't be involved in this. She was an innocent in the wrong place at the wrong time…married to the wrong man.

Her fingers crept up his shirt to cradle his jaw. The touch was sweet, yet excruciatingly painful.

"Kyle, I—" Her voice cracked.

Her breath warmed his stubbled jaw. She was so close and smelled so good.

They were probably both about to be captured and killed yet all he could think about was kissing her. People do strange things in the face of danger, incredible, unpredictable things.

She leaned forward and kissed his cheek, the warmth filling his chest. She was relieved, that's all, grateful for the rescue.

Soldiers' voices bounced off the rocks. "There, on the other side of that boulder. I heard something!"

Kyle held her away from him and struggled to sharpen his survival instincts dulled by his desire. He brushed a kiss against her lips, figuring it would be his last, sprang from their secluded spot and charged the soldiers.

Chapter Seven

"What the hell?" the older soldier swore as Kyle shouldered him in the chest.

Kyle pinned the guy and started punching until the younger guy managed to pull him off. The soldier's firm neck hold pressed against Kyle's windpipe, cutting off air.

Hell, he needed to move this wrestling match away from Andrea's hiding spot before they discovered her.

The older soldier, a middle-aged, husky guy, got up, his eyes flaring with rage. He dusted off his army fatigues and smiled.

"I'll bet you're McKendrick," he said. "I'm Private Dilling."

With a tight fist, he slugged Kyle, once, twice. By the third blow, Kyle's body wanted to curl into itself but the younger soldier held him upright as Dilling used his stomach as a punching bag. Dilling leaned close to Kyle's ear.

"We're looking for the woman. We'll end this right here if you tell us where she is. We've got plans for her," he said with a wink.

Kyle'd kill them before he'd let them touch her.

"I hear she's a fine piece," Dilling taunted. "Could be fun to have around for a while, until we turn her over to the major."

If he wanted a reaction he wasn't about to get it. Letting on to his feelings for Andrea would put her in more danger.

Kyle pulled at the younger soldier's arm to release the pressure. "She's gone," he rasped.

"You wouldn't be lying to us, would you?"

"Haven't…haven't seen her since yesterday," he croaked.

"I'll bet you've got her hidden somewhere, keeping her all to yourself. That isn't very soldier-like. We've been without women for way too long, isn't that right, Babcock?"

No one would touch her, not like that. Kyle kicked the young soldier in the shin and the kid loosened his grip long enough for Kyle to elbow him in the ribs. The punk let go and Kyle charged.

Head down, shoulders ready for impact, Kyle dove at Dilling and they both tumbled over the edge of the ridge. Dilling didn't have time to aim his gun and shoot. Jaw clenched, Kyle rolled down the mountainside, gritting his teeth with each bump. He came to a stop, his body screaming in pain but charged with adrenaline. He looked up into the barrel of a pistol.

"Well, well. What's all this?"

Kyle recognized Lieutenant John Crane, a loyal soldier who excelled at taking orders.

"That sonofabitch!" Dilling cried, storming toward them.

"Back off, Private," Crane said. "We need information first."

"I'll find out what you need to know." Dilling fisted his hand.

"I'd like to interrogate him myself," Crane said. "Where's Babcock?"

"Here, sir!" the soldier answered, coming down the ridge.

Alone. Kyle breathed a sigh of relief. His plan had worked. They hadn't found her.

Get the hell out of here, Andy.

"Take him into my tent and secure him," Crane ordered.

"Yes, sir," the younger soldier said. They pulled Kyle to his feet and dragged him to the tent.

"I'll take care of it." Dilling dismissed the punk, then delivered a full-fisted punch to Kyle's gut.

"Not so tough now." He shoved Kyle into a chair, cuffed his hands in front and secured his ankles to the chair legs with a thick rope.

"Don't want you running off again. Biehl is looking forward to a nice, long talk with you. I hope I'm around to help…you know, take notes," the soldier said, a threatening tone to his voice. "Oh, one more thing…" He towered over Kyle and waited.

Kyle glanced up and the bastard delivered a right cross that shot stars across his line of vision. Dilling smiled and left the tent.

Pulling against his leg restraints, Kyle fought back the frustration that he'd ended up right where he'd started. He hoped Andrea was safe. He could deal with anything if he knew she was okay.

He could deal with anything if he knew she was okay?

What was happening to him? He was starting to care too much about this woman. It was obligation that drove him, he told himself. He had to protect Jimmy's wife. Yet by protecting her he'd put his life on the line and failed at finding the evidence to nail Biehl.

Someone entered the tent. Kyle pinched his eyes shut, hoping if he pretended to be unconscious they'd leave him alone and give him time to plan a way out of this.

"McKendrick?"

He glanced up. Lieutenant Crane stood over him, and for a minute Kyle thought the real beating was about to begin. Instead, a puzzled expression creased the older man's forehead.

Crane had aged plenty since he and Kyle had worked together. Worry lines stretched across the lieutenant's face and his hair had turned from a distinguished salt-and-pepper to a silver-gray. Crane pulled out a metal flask and handed it to Kyle.

"You look like you could use this," he said.

Kyle eyed the flask with suspicion.

"Don't worry, it's whiskey." He pulled up a stool.

He and Crane had been on assignment a few years ago and had drunk themselves into oblivion in celebration of a successful rescue. Crane had nearly been killed in that one.

"I guess I could use some of that," Kyle admitted.

Crane reached out and turned Kyle's face one way, then the other, examining his soldier's handiwork. "New recruits. A bit overzealous. I am surprised they got the best of you, what with your reputation."

Did Crane suspect Kyle had sacrificed himself on purpose? With bound wrists, he took the flask and swallowed a shot. The liquor burned its way down his chest.

"Remember the last time we shared a drink?" Crane said.

"Seems like a lifetime ago."

"You've dug yourself quite a hole, my friend."

Kyle studied the flask, dented and rusted. Reminded him of his life.

Crane leaned forward. "What the hell did you do to get Biehl so pissed off? The word is, 'dead or alive,' although he made it clear he'd prefer alive so he can kill you himself."

"Sounds like Biehl."

"Mac, talk to me."

The compassion in the man's voice reminded Kyle of his own father and his soft-spoken ways, his wise lectures about the fragility of women and the importance of discipline. For a minute, he wished for the hand of an older, wiser man to help him out of this mess.

Then he remembered: there was no way out.

"Jimmy…" Kyle began, his voice catching on his friend's name. "You heard about Jimmy Franks."

"I heard he was killed, something about getting in the line of fire. Biehl uses it as an example. Says if Jimmy had followed orders he'd be alive today."

"That sonofabitch," he muttered. "It didn't go down like that." He took a deep breath, staring into Crane's gray eyes. "Biehl set him up to die on purpose."

Crane sat back in his chair as if he didn't believe him.

"We were hired to get the Donohue family out of South America," Kyle rambled. "Only there was no Donohue family. It was a set-up."

"I don't understand. Biehl said—"

"He lied. Jimmy had evidence on Biehl that could destroy him. If he didn't turn it over to the major…" His voice weakened, the guilt of his friend's death clawing at his insides.

"Jimmy would die at the hands of the enemy?" Crane offered.

Kyle nodded.

"But I heard Jimmy was shot by one of our own."

"I shot him."

The words encased his heart like black ice. A heart he could never share with another soul. Especially not Jimmy's widow.

"Why?" Crane said in disbelief.

"They'd strapped him to a post. They were about to cut him. I…I had no choice," he said, struggling against the guilt, the grief.

"I'm sorry. I know you and Jimmy were close," the older man said, his tone soft.

A few minutes of silence passed. Crane stood and paced the twelve-foot tent. "I've suspected that Biehl is a megalomaniac, but I didn't know he'd sacrifice one of his own men." He looked at Kyle. "What does he want with you?"

"He thinks I know where the evidence is that can bring him down."

"Do you?"

He hesitated. Could Crane be manipulating him,

giving him whiskey and reminiscing about old times to
get information?

"I've got leads, but I don't know for sure."

"And the woman? What's her role in this?"

"She's Jimmy's wife."

"Holy…" Crane's voice trailed off. "What do you
think the major will do once he gets his hands on her?"

Kyle shrugged, biting back the agony that threatened
to swallow him whole. He wanted desperately to live so
he could protect her from Biehl's sadistic games.

"Biehl wants the evidence and if he can't find it,
he'll kill anyone who might have access to it."

Crane sat down. "But Jimmy died years ago. Why is
this coming to a head now?"

"After I…after Jimmy died, I was messed up.
When I got my act together, I told the major I wanted
out. He said there is no quitting unless he approves
it. Biehl started a fire in my parents' house to make
his point."

"What the hell?" Crane whispered.

"He had me, and he knew it. The guilt over what I'd
done to Jimmy was unbearable, but my hatred for Biehl
was worse. He made me kill my best friend. He threatened my family. I acted the obedient soldier until I saw
the opportunity to take him down. My investigation
brought me to Colorado."

"You know there's a rumor he's pushing for a pro-
motion?"

Kyle shook his head. "So, that's why he's so desperate to make this problem disappear."

"Any idea on the whereabouts of the evidence?"

"I was chasing a lead when Biehl caught me, drugged me and locked me up in The Lab."

Crane's face went white. "I've heard about that place. That's where they work on prisoners."

"They messed with my head in the hopes of finding out what I knew. There was a guy there, someone who also wanted out. He told me about a cabin in the Rockies and helped me escape. I didn't know it was a set-up."

"How do you mean?"

"They sent me straight to Andrea Franks's cabin for the supposed evidence. The major knew what it would do to me to be around the woman I'd widowed, and he figured she'd have good reason to kill me if she found out what I'd done."

"But she hasn't killed you."

Kyle glanced at him. "No."

She'd had plenty of opportunities to let him die, or kill him.

Crane motioned for Kyle to take a swig of whiskey.

"I'll never forget when we escaped those bastards in Iraq," Crane said.

Kyle nodded.

"We were so full of ourselves, so cocky..." Crane's gaze drifted to the floor. "We did good things back then. What the hell happened?"

Kyle shook his head.

"I don't have anything against Biehl," Crane said. "He seems to respect my opinion, gives me pretty easy assignments now that I'm getting old." He pointed to his silver hair.

"Old man," Kyle said with a smile.

"Yeah, well, your day will come." He leaned back in his chair and crossed one leg over the other. "Lately, I've seen the way Major Biehl trains these kids, running them into the ground, beating on them. He makes them mean."

Kyle remembered Jimmy's dark moods, his violent temper, and wondered what scars those moods had left on Andrea.

Crane sipped his whiskey. "I've heard he uses soldiers' families to keep them in line, that he won't let anyone leave the Force."

"Yes." Kyle struggled with the image of his sister bound to a wheelchair, fighting to get out of a burning house.

"When I signed on I thought Beta Force was an extension of the military," Crane said. "When I suspected otherwise I confronted the major. He said there are things the American people want done, but won't admit to wanting done. Major Biehl said the U.S. needs Beta Force to do those things, go in where the President wouldn't send regular military. At the time it made sense. But now, I don't know. I'm thinking Beta Force was designed as the major's personal militia."

Kyle took another swig. The whiskey was getting to him, his wound no longer screamed and his eye no longer throbbed. His shoulder muscles unclenched.

"I didn't sign on for this," Crane muttered. "Four men were killed last month. The major seemed aloof when I talked to him about it. A true military leader would never be so casual about losing his men."

"He's over the edge," Kyle said, remembering the way he'd backhanded Andrea, and how he'd beat his own soldier for his incompetence. He took another swig of whiskey.

Crane shifted closer. "What do you know about the missing evidence?"

"Not much. I think there are photographs, maybe pages from his infamous notebook. The egomaniac probably thinks it will go on display in some museum or something. It's got dates and illegal missions. I'm telling you, he's lost it. Jimmy was Biehl's assistant for a while and read a few pages. He said there was enough in there to open an investigation. Biehl would probably be dishonorably discharged at the least."

"And the rest of us?"

Kyle read worry in the older man's eyes. "I'm not sure. I'm trying to help men who are forced to kill because of Biehl's threats against their families. I don't know what that means for the rest of us."

Nor did he care what happened to him. His life had ended the day he'd killed his friend.

"Kyle?"

He glanced at Crane.

"About Iraq…"

"Forget it."

"I'm still breathing because of you," Crane said.

"You would have done the same."

"Don't be so sure," the lieutenant joked. His smile faded and silence blanketed the tent.

"As I see it, son, you've got two choices," Crane said. "You can either come back with us to face the major, or die here in the Rockies."

Kyle's heart raced. The last fifteen minutes had given

him hope. He'd thought maybe he'd found an ally, a sympathizer in his cause.

Instead, he would die without completing his mission. Without helping Andrea, protecting her…

Making love to her.

He closed his eyes. The whiskey had really loosened his inhibitions to be thinking in that direction. Hell, why not enjoy the last few minutes of his life by fantasizing about something he'd never have: a beautiful, loving woman?

Crane cleared his throat and Kyle opened his eyes.

"Knowing Biehl, I'd choose death if I were you," he offered.

"You'll be the one to pull the trigger?" Kyle asked, not wanting either of the cocky jerks outside to take him down.

"If that's what you want."

"It is."

WITHOUT THINKING, Andrea did as ordered and ran.

Like a coward.

What else was she supposed to do? She wasn't trained to fight these mercenaries.

She hadn't gone very far when the guilt stopped her. They'd taken Kyle. And done what? Beaten him for information about her? Killed him? He wouldn't give up without one helluva fight.

His words haunted her: *If something happens to me, you get the hell out of here.*

He'd planned this, planned to jump out of hiding and divert attention away from Andrea. He was protecting her.

She'd run from Jamison's cabin, yet Kyle had tracked

her down and saved her, comforted her and sacrificed himself to the enemy. For her.

No, this was about his guilt over killing Jimmy. *I couldn't let him die like that.*

But Jimmy had been emotionally dead to her for the last year of his life. She couldn't save Jimmy, couldn't protect her nephew and now would be the cause of Kyle's death.

No, she wouldn't let that happen. She had to stop running, and she had to go back and help him. For all the reasons she knew, and some she didn't.

For a split second, she wished she were the agent Kyle had accused her of being when he'd first showed up at the cabin. That agent would know what to do.

She rubbed her hands together to warm them and began to formulate a plan. A diversion? Call the local cops? Kyle would be safer with them than Biehl, right? Then again Biehl had convinced everyone that Kyle was a child killer.

She found a secluded spot and motioned for the dogs. The three of them huddled together to keep warm.

Andrea clicked off one plan after another, in much the same way she had done when she'd tried to bring Jimmy out of his funk. She'd tried to get him to talk to his brother, she'd pushed marital counseling and even suggested he be tested for depression.

Jimmy had refused all of her ideas. She hadn't been able to save him. But maybe, with a bit of luck, she could save McKendrick. Why? Because he'd saved her multiple times?

No, because the guilt she'd read in his golden-brown

eyes matched her own. That connection prevented her from abandoning him to certain death.

She could navigate the mountains better than these soldiers. All she needed to do was sneak into their camp, disable their vehicle and free McKendrick. The agents would be stuck until help arrived, giving Andrea and Kyle time to escape.

She hiked back to the ridge above the campsite.

One man was sitting beside the campfire, the other stood guard on the perimeter. She spied a truck parked backwards, probably to make it easier to unload their equipment. Perfect.

"I should have killed you in Argentina, you sonofa-bitch!" A gray-haired soldier pulled Kyle out of the tent and shoved him to the ground.

Daisy growled.

"Shush," Andrea said.

"Get up when I'm talking to you!"

Kyle stood and stumbled, his hands bound by the cuffs.

"You low-life, arrogant, disloyal jerk!" The man backhanded Kyle. He went face-down into the dirt.

Andrea fisted her hands. The other two soldiers watched the beating as if it was their entertainment for the evening. Jerks.

She scrambled closer, shielding herself behind a spruce tree.

"Get up, McKendrick!"

Kyle pushed up off the ground and stood tall. He held out his hands. "You want a fair fight? Uncuff me."

The officer motioned to one of his men. "Do it."

"But sir," the soldier protested.

"That's an order, private. McKendrick and I have unfinished business."

The soldier removed the cuffs and the officer whipped off his uniform jacket and crooked his finger at Kyle.

Her pulse raced.

Helpless again. No, no. Fight it. Use this diversion to make your move. She edged her way down to the truck, determined to stay focused and disable their vehicle.

A lot of good it would do her if Kyle was beaten to death.

"You're so smart, had to have it your way," the older man shouted.

The other two soldiers were distracted by the fight and wouldn't sense her approach.

She removed her backpack for better mobility, and took out her knife. With silent steps, she edged closer, sticking to the cover of trees.

It was maybe twenty feet to the truck. She peeked around a pine tree and saw Kyle charge the gray-haired man. They both went down, fists flying as they tumbled in a haze of fury. The two soldiers shouted encouragement to their superior officer.

She took slow, deep breaths and waited.

"You stupid bastard!" The older man slugged Kyle in the stomach.

She didn't want to watch, but couldn't turn away— she needed to be ready for her opportunity.

The soldier stood and kicked Kyle twice. He didn't move.

Good, play dead so he'll stop beating you.

The officer walked back to the campfire and warmed his hands over the flame. "What the hell happens to make a man so pathetic?" The guy motioned for one of the soldiers to pass him something.

They were going to shoot him?

Instead, the soldier offered up cigars.

"Biehl will reward us all for catching this coward." The officer clipped the tips of three cigars and passed them out, then held out the lighter.

She edged closer…a little closer.

Suddenly Kyle got up and broke into a sprint. What the heck?

The soldiers started after him. Andrea raced to the truck, stabbed two of the tires with her knife and darted back to cover.

"Dilling, Babcock, stop!" **the** silver-haired officer ordered.

Oh, God, had they seen her? She didn't dare look.

Two shots rang out.

She ducked as her heart leapt into her throat. She turned and dashed through the rough terrain, branches whipping her cheeks. She approached the edge of a clearing and spun around in time to see the three men peering over a steep drop.

Her breath caught when she realized they weren't shooting at her. They'd been shooting at Kyle, who must have plummeted down the mountainside.

"Where'd he go?" a soldier asked.

"Down there," the officer answered. "Get me a rifle."

The soldier got a long-barreled rifle from the tent and brought it to his commanding officer.

Using the trees for cover, she got closer to the ridge, hoping she'd look down and Kyle would be gone. Instead, the moonlight illuminated his motionless body. He looked dead, yet the officer planned to shoot him anyway?

"No," she whispered, panic consuming her.

Kyle was bad...and he was good. He protected Andrea, made her feel...things. She had closed herself off since her marriage fell apart. She wasn't supposed to feel anything ever again.

But she did. She felt anger, frustration...and compassion for Kyle McKendrick.

Chewing on his cigar, the officer aimed the rifle at Kyle.

Her eyes darted from the scene below to the dogs perched on the ridge. She motioned for them to join her, quickly, while the soldiers were focused on their task.

Killing Kyle.

No, Biehl wanted him alive, right?

She couldn't save Jimmy, couldn't save Kyle. She had to stop the officer. She had to—

The officer fired three shots at Kyle's body. Her shoulders jerked and her legs weakened. She crumbled to the ground as the dogs raced to her side.

"Sir, should we drag him up here?" a soldier asked.

"It will be light soon. We'll get him then. If there's anything left. Mountain animals love fresh meat." The soldiers laughed as they walked away, smoking their cigars.

Kyle. Dead. She couldn't prevent it, couldn't save him. She struggled to breathe, but her lungs wouldn't fill.

Staring blindly at the dark sky that had always brought her peace, she realized that tonight it resembled a shroud.

Jimmy, why so much death? She fought back tears.

She'd given up crying after Jimmy had died, after she had found out what he really was. She had denied her emotions and buried her feelings so deep that some days she wondered if she was still alive.

The pain slicing her heart answered that question. She'd tried desperately to keep anyone from getting through, but she'd connected to Kyle McKendrick.

Daisy's ears pricked and she raced down the steep mountainside toward Kyle.

"Daisy, no!" Andrea whispered. She knew where Daisy was going. Andrea had the same urge, but couldn't risk being caught. She scanned the camp. The men sat by the campfire, laughing and drinking, while Kyle lay at the bottom of a canyon, his body bullet-riddled.

She followed Daisy. The dog had grown attached to Kyle. Andrea had grown attached to Kyle, although she hated to admit it. She remembered Kyle's rescue, offering his hand...the kiss. She hadn't been physically that close to another man since before Jimmy had died. The thought had never crossed her mind.

She'd wanted to kiss Kyle. And not just on the cheek.

"Daisy," she whispered, following the dog down the steep path. When she finally caught up with her, Daisy whined and paced over to Kyle's lifeless body. Sprawled on his back, he didn't look anything like the man whose wounds Andrea had tended last night. His face was smudged with dirt, his hands were bloodied and raw.

With sheer determination he'd saved her from Biehl's

death soldiers more than once. And now he looked like a rag doll torn at the seams.

"Oh, God." Her hand shot up to cover her mouth as the words escaped her lips. "Daisy, honey. We can't stay here. I'm sorry, I'm so sorry."

Daisy whined, lay down and put her head on his chest. Andrea spotted dark-red blood seeping through the shirt she'd given him. She had to get out of here or she'd fall apart.

"Daisy, we've got to go. We can't help him, baby."

The golden retriever wouldn't budge.

Andrea knelt beside him and touched his cheek with her fingertips. If only—

"I told you to get the hell away from here." Kyle's eyes shot open and he clamped his hand over her mouth.

Chapter Eight

Kyle removed his hand and Andrea stared at him, speechless.

"Breathe, Andrea," he whispered.

"You're dead," she gasped, reaching over to touch him.

"I'll explain later. I hear water over there, beyond those trees."

She couldn't speak, her emotions tangled around her vocal chords.

"Take my arms and drag me over there," he said. "Can you do that? Are you strong enough?"

He extended his arms and closed his eyes as if preparing himself for the pain of being dragged across the rocky terrain. But why didn't he get up and walk? Was he paralyzed?

"Kyle, I—"

He opened his eyes. "Andrea, please do what I ask. We don't have much time."

Grabbing his wrists, she tugged in short, quick jerks. The stream looked twenty feet away, but felt more like twenty miles. She dragged him half way, then collapsed, kneeling beside him.

"I have to…" she gasped for air, "take a second to…"

He reached out and touched her cheek. "You're doing fine. You can do it, I know you can."

She straightened and grabbed his arms. With renewed strength she pulled him another ten feet to the stream. She knelt beside him. "Oh, Kyle, I'm so sorry."

"Andrea. Stop. Look at me."

She glanced up. Determined dark eyes stared back at her. "You're not done. Drag me into the water."

"But—"

"Now," he demanded.

She stepped away from him. He obviously had given up hope. "You're going to…to drown yourself?"

"No, just do it."

He extended his arms but she hesitated, unsure what to do.

"C'mon sweetheart."

The endearment melted her insides. She couldn't remember the last time a man had spoken to her with such gentleness.

"Trust me," he said.

She grabbed his arms and dragged him until his entire body was submersed in water. The stream wasn't deep but the frigid water numbed her feet and calves. She cradled his head in her hands to keep it above the water's surface. He wasn't about to kill himself, not with her standing there.

"Let go, Andrea."

"No."

With a splash, he rolled onto his knees and pushed up to a standing position. Soaked to the skin, beaten and bruised, she should have felt sorry for him. Instead, she was furious.

"I thought you were paralyzed." She shoved at his chest and the palm of her hand met with hard metal. "What the heck?"

"Beat me up later. Right now we have to make this look good. Get Oscar over here."

"Why?"

"Just this once, please, don't ask questions and call the dog over here."

His impatient expression almost had her laughing hysterically. She'd gladly choose impatience over death. Kyle was alive. Relief rolled across her shoulders.

"Oscar, come," she whispered.

Kyle stripped off his shirt to reveal a chest plate.

"What is that?" she asked.

"New light armor. Bulletproof." He tapped it with his knuckles.

She edged closer and saw two bullets embedded in the metal. He unbuckled the armor and placed it on the ground. Blood seeped down the side of his chest from the shoulder wound. Two marks centered his chest where bullets had embedded in the metal and bruised his skin.

"Whoa," she said, touching the marks in fascination.

"Uh, how about a rain check?" he joked.

She jerked her hand away, embarrassed.

He dangled his shirt in Oscar's face. "You've always wanted a piece of me. Here's your chance. C'mon, grab it, that a boy."

She watched in disbelief as Kyle and Oscar played

tug-of-war in the middle of a frigid mountain stream with Biehl's men sitting around a campfire on the ridge above. The soldiers had beaten him senseless. That was the only explanation for his behavior.

"All right, not bad," he said, rubbing the dog's ears. "Good job, buddy." He tossed the mutilated shirt to the edge of the creek, picked up the armor and turned to her. "Let's go."

"You sure? I mean he's even better with denim," she said, glancing at Kyle's jeans.

"You'd like that, wouldn't you?" He grabbed her hand. "C'mon."

As he pulled her along, she noticed he wasn't gripping her wrist, or squeezing her arm. He was holding her hand.

"Where's your backpack?"

"Up there." She pointed.

"I'd better get it. Take cover behind those trees and wait for me."

"I'd rather come with you."

Stopping short, he turned on her and she collided into his naked chest. Even bruised and battered it radiated strength.

"I realize you aren't one for taking orders or relying on other people," he said. "But can you trust that I know what I'm doing?"

She opened her mouth to argue and he squeezed her hand. That small gesture meant more to her than his orders.

"Be right back." He turned and started for the backpack.

"Kyle?" she whispered.

He glanced over his shoulder and smiled, a smile that

lit her insides from her hairline to her toes. She smiled back. It struck her that she'd never seen him smile, not that he had much to smile about. It was a fascinating expression, the corners of his mouth turning up slightly, as though he had secret.

She crouched beside a tree and stroked Oscar, then gave Daisy an extra-big hug. If it hadn't been for Daisy's determination Andrea would have whispered her good-byes to a lifeless Kyle McKendrick from afar, never knowing he was still breathing.

Boy did he breathe well, she thought, remembering the broad chest she'd touched when exploring the bullet marks. Traveling with a half-naked Kyle McKendrick would be her undoing. Then again, maybe she could convince him that a little romp in the wilderness wasn't such a bad idea.

Where did that come from? It must be the aftereffects of an adrenaline rush, followed by grief, followed by relief. Her emotions were all over the place.

And she felt way too vulnerable.

When he reappeared with her backpack she felt a little less so, but she scolded herself for her sexual fantasy. Blood seeped from his lip and a goose egg had formed above his right eye. This man needed a week in the hospital, not a night of crazed sex with a woman he barely knew.

"Let's get moving," he said.

"How's the shoulder?"

"We'll stop to take care of my aches and pains later."

"But if you—"

He flashed his index finger in her face.

"Right," she said. "Don't argue."

He turned and started up the mountain. She hiked behind him, studying his broad shoulders tapering to a trim waist. It frightened her that she craved more than a simple touch from this man, this mercenary whose life revolved around violence and death. Against her own wishes, her heart had opened up to Kyle.

How sick was that?

Oscar trotted close to Andrea, not completely sold on Kyle's integrity. Dogs have instincts, she reminded herself, instincts about whether a person is good or bad. She glanced at Daisy who trotted beside Kyle. So much for that theory.

"Pick up the pace," he said. "We've got to get as far away from here as we can." He hid the armor beneath a juniper bush and reached for her hand. "You okay?"

He was bruised and bleeding and he wanted to know if she was okay. Physically she was fine. Her emotions, on the other hand, were a mess.

"I'm fine," she lied, struggling to keep her mind off his warm and gentle hand. "Why not keep the armor?"

"If they find it on me they'll know Crane helped me escape. I wouldn't do that to him."

Once again he was concerned about someone else's safety.

"Lieutenant Crane gave me this to keep track of Biehl's whereabouts." He pulled a small radio from his jeans pocket. "I hope it wasn't ruined when I took the header over the cliff."

"Why would he help you?"

"I saved his life once, and he felt he owed me."

"After he beat you up," she said, anger filling her voice.

He squeezed her hand and she looked into his dark eyes. Her breath caught. "It was all part of the game," he said.

"A game," she muttered, wondering where the game ended and reality began.

They walked in silence for miles, through the thick brush, up one trail, down another and along a creek. Her feet grew numb and her cheeks chilled. She couldn't begin to imagine how he felt, naked from the waist up, the crisp mountain breeze slapping his chest.

"Hey, wait." She pulled him to a stop.

"Andrea, this is no time to—"

"A shirt, I have a shirt." She dug in her backpack and pulled out her long-sleeved, cotton nightshirt.

"This might work. You look…cold." Her words caught in her throat and she hoped he didn't sense her physical attraction to him. This was getting way too complicated.

"WOMEN'S CLOTHING," he said. "What will the guys think?"

She smiled and Kyle took a step back. Why was it that every time she did that, a part of him wanted to reach out and brush his fingers across her lips, to absorb her warmth into his skin?

"Before you put the shirt on, let me take care of that shoulder wound," she said.

"Later."

"Now."

That determined set to her jaw told him he wasn't going anywhere until she checked his injury. Giving in, he sat on a rock, clutching the shirt in his hand. He dreaded her gentle touch, yet he craved it with an intensity that scared the crap out of him.

"It will never be over, will it?" she asked, applying ointment to his wound. Her fingers felt wonderful against his skin, and for a second he wanted to lie and tell her that this nightmare had a happy ending.

It didn't. Not for Andrea, who'd lost her husband, and certainly not for Kyle, whose soul had been permanently scarred. He couldn't change the bad decision he'd made to join the Force, nor could he change what he'd become. But he could change the stranglehold Biehl had over innocent young men.

"There's only one way to end it," he said.

"Destroy Biehl."

He nodded, closing his eyes. He focused on her long, steady strokes that reached far deeper than the top layer of his skin. She applied the bandage, rubbing her thumbs across the adhesive to secure it.

"Then there is no end," she said.

He opened his eyes. "Why do you say that?"

"Biehl is well-respected. No one would believe us."

"You've got to have faith."

"I wish I could." She glanced at the gauze in her hand. "Jimmy's parents were told he died honorably. It would destroy them to find out he was part of some secret army that kills for sport."

"It didn't start out that way," he said.

He pushed aside the image of his own parents, the two people he respected most in the world. The two people whose hearts were probably breaking from the news that Kyle was wanted for murdering two children.

There was always the chance word hadn't reached his hometown of Sterling, Illinois.

"Sometimes things have to die to be reborn," he whispered.

She shot him a puzzled expression.

"C'mon. Let's keep moving." He stood and extended his hand.

"Take some of this first." She fished a small bottle out of her pack and placed a few drops of liquid onto his tongue. "It will help heal the shoulder wound."

Her simple touch, her concern, was healing something deeper inside his chest.

She put away her supplies and took his hand. They continued their hike, flanked by the dogs. The heat from her skin weaved its way into his heart, and he knew that once it settled there, he'd never be the same. He cautioned himself to keep his emotional distance from this woman. She'd been hurt in far too many ways by someone like Kyle. She didn't need another disappointment. He knew, deep down, he couldn't give her what she needed most. He pulled his hand away.

"Do you want me to carry the pack for a while?" he asked, not sure how his shoulder would endure the chivalrous gesture.

"No, thanks. How are all the cuts and bruises?" she asked, eyeing him.

His body lit with awareness. "I'll make it."

"Maybe I should check," she said, studying a cut on his arm as they walked.

"No, don't." He pulled away, her touch driving him mad.

Hell, he still couldn't believe she was here with him. He'd ordered her to escape with her life, to leave him behind. Instead she'd followed him and risked her life. If the soldiers had spotted her, gotten their hands on her...

He slowed down and she looked at him in question.

"Why didn't you run like I ordered you to?" he said.

"You saved me and I had to return the favor."

"By doing what? You're not a commando."

"I slashed their tires," she offered.

"Good God, Andrea. You were that close?"

She nodded.

"Never do that again." He gently gripped her by the shoulders. "Promise me?"

"But I owe you."

"You owe me nothing, Andrea, especially considering what I've done."

"I remember." She clenched her jaw.

Good, he'd brought the pain to the surface, reminded her that he was evil to the core.

"I need to get to a phone to warn my brother-in-law." She took off ahead of him.

He reined in his temper as he followed close behind. She'd been determined to save him, even if that meant putting herself in harm's way.

That was foolish and stupid. Yet he liked the thought that someone cared that much about him.

She didn't care, not really. It had to be gratitude, that's all. But he'd seen tears in her eyes when she'd thought him dead. He guessed it took a lot to make this strong woman cry.

He quickened his pace. Andrea was getting under his skin, and that could be deadly for them both.

They traveled in angry silence for hours. She had to be exhausted. "Let's take a break," he said.

"But Biehl's men—"

"Think I'm dead. Besides, they're not going anywhere since you disabled their vehicle." He shot her a half smile, which she did not return. "We haven't slept all night. Let's rest for a couple of hours. There, by those trees."

She nodded and headed toward cover. She still hadn't looked at him. Just as well. If those eyes caught his heart one more time, he might lose his resolve to keep his hands off of her.

AN HOUR LATER, they sat beside a small campfire and shared what was left of the dry food. They'd strategically placed themselves on either side of the fire, Oscar staying close to Andrea while Daisy had settled her head on Kyle's thigh.

Kyle studied the fire and welcomed the silence. It had been one of the longest days of his life, running from Biehl's men, trying to keep his hands off his friend's wife.

She'd cast a spell on him from the first time he'd seen her. His heart had been hooked and reeled in like a trout that had nibbled the wrong line. He glanced up and caught her staring at him.

He tensed. "What?"

She shook her head and stared at burning embers.

He'd give anything to know what went on in that

mind of hers, what she thought about when she stared at the fluid movement of the flames.

"C'mon, what?" he pushed.

She looked up and his heart skipped a beat at her wistful expression. "Jimmy used to love to camp," she said. "He made great camp fires."

Kyle's heart ripped in two. *She's not thinking about you, fool. She's thinking about her dead husband, the man she loved.*

"Did you ever go camping with him?" she asked.

"Yeah." He paused, wondering if it would help her or hurt her to talk about Jimmy.

"Tell me about it."

"We were sent into the Smoky Mountains once to locate a crazed militia group. Jimmy decided to make the biggest fire east of the Mississippi."

"Wouldn't the bad guys find you?" she asked.

The bad guys. She actually didn't put Kyle in that category.

"We'd completed the mission. Anyway, we were celebrating, drinking, and Jimmy decides, 'Hey, let's pour whiskey on the fire and see how big it gets.' He was holding homemade moonshine we'd taken off some locals."

"He did have a reckless streak," she whispered, hugging her knees to her chest.

Had he gone too far and made her uncomfortable? "I'm sorry…I shouldn't have—"

"Sure you should. It's nice to talk about him like this. It's been so long since I've been able even to think about Jimmy. At the end, he ruined all the good memories for me."

She gazed into the fire and he wanted to hold her, to convince her that Jimmy had always loved her even when he didn't act like it.

"What else do you remember?" she asked.

He searched his mind for the good stuff. "His sense of humor." He paused. "And the way his eyes lit up when he talked about you."

She stared at the fire.

"Your turn," he encouraged, hoping he was doing the right thing.

She hugged her knees a little tighter. "I'll never forget the time we sneaked out after prom. We found a quiet spot on the beach. All we wanted was to lie in each other's arms and talk."

Her expression grew distant. Was she remembering how it felt to be held by the man she loved? The pain of having lost that connection must be unbearable.

"Anyway, we're lying there, eyes closed, talking about the future, marriage and kids." She stopped, as if recalling the memory.

"And? What happened?"

She glanced up as if she'd completely forgotten his presence. "A light shines in our face. Jimmy says, 'The night flies when you're in my arms.' He thought it was the sunrise, but it was a local cop pointing a flashlight at us. I was petrified, but not Jimmy. He knew he'd get us out of trouble. If my folks had ever found out I would have been grounded for life."

"They didn't like Jimmy?"

"Oh, they loved Jimmy. They didn't tolerate lying. They worried a lot about me. I was kind of a naive kid.

Jimmy was my protector, especially after my parents moved away."

"What happened with the cop?" he said, shifting onto his side.

"You know Jimmy. He charmed the cop with some ridiculous story. We got a lecture and were ordered to go home. Jimmy was good at getting out of tight spots." She paused. "He was good at a lot of things."

A minute of silence passed. She ran her hand down Oscar's back. He stretched and grunted.

"I hardly knew him in the end," she said. "One day I woke up and didn't recognize the man I'd married."

"But he was still Jimmy. He was still a good person, deep down."

"He wasn't always so good to me."

Kyle sat up, his heart slamming against his chest. "Tell me he didn't hit you."

She looked away. "Not really."

He knew what "not really" meant. It meant yes. He wanted to scream, break something. How could Jimmy have raised a hand to this beautiful creature? She was kind and gentle, compassionate and giving. Jimmy had described her as the most precious thing in his life.

Then Kyle remembered how Jimmy's moods had grown dark in the end. Kyle had suggested he get professional help before he did something he'd regret. Why didn't she leave him before it came to physical abuse?

He glanced across the fire and noticed her swipe at her eyes.

"Andrea," he said, going to her.

"No, no, I'm fine." She put out her hand. "Smoke from the campfire made my eyes water."

He sat beside her anyway and pulled her against his chest. "Well, I'm cold so warm me up."

He held her close, like the time he'd held Jimmy when they were thrown into a cell in Colombia. Jimmy had shivered, scared of dying, terrified of being tortured.

It was after that torture and subsequent rescue that the emptiness had invaded Jimmy's eyes, an emptiness Kyle couldn't replace with hope no matter how hard he'd tried.

"I'm really okay." She pushed away from Kyle. "Sorry I keep clinging to you like a security blanket."

"Don't be sorry. You loved him. He loved you."

She slipped a strand of black hair behind her ear. "If he really loved me I wouldn't have lost him the way I did."

He cradled her face between his hands, forcing her to look at him. "It's not your fault."

He read disbelief in her eyes. She turned away from him and stood, pacing a few feet away.

Damn, why wouldn't she let him comfort her? *Kind of a dumb question, Mac.*

"I will not let Jimmy's family be hurt because of me, because I didn't warn them. That's why I need to get to a phone."

"When the sun comes up we'll deal with that." He went back to his side of the fire where he was safe from her vulnerability, and stretched out on his back. "Using a public phone is dangerous. Can you think of anyone you'd trust with your life?"

"Clint and Ricky's dad, Henry," she offered.

"Great, those bozos would love to get another shot at me."

"They're good people. They care about me."

I care about you.

He wouldn't say it; couldn't say it. He didn't want to further complicate her life. He needed to get her safe and continue his search for the evidence against Biehl.

"I'm glad you're not dead," she said from across the fire.

He turned and studied her bright-green eyes. He was sliding into that gray zone where emotions were clouding his better judgment.

"Get some sleep," he said.

For once she didn't argue. She curled up, her sweet face lit by the dancing flames. Yes, he could see why Jimmy loved her so much. She was beautiful, inside and out.

And he'd do anything to protect the woman who'd opened a part of his heart that he had thought destroyed years ago.

Chapter Nine

They approached Henry Simpson's property and relief coursed through Andrea's body. It had been a long journey back, and Kyle had been quiet most of the way. She'd asked about his shoulder wound, but he'd dismissed her inquiry. It almost seemed as if they were strangers again.

"Did I do something?" she blurted out.

"I'm sorry?"

"To upset you."

"No."

End of conversation.

"Is that it?" he asked, pointing at the Simpson house.

"Yep."

"They've got a working phone?"

"They do."

"Good, call Jimmy's brother but keep it short. You don't want Biehl to trace the call."

He scanned the property from the trail. "Looks safe. I'll go in first. If Biehl's men are hiding, I'll draw them out." He eyed her. "You stay back, hear me? If Biehl's men show up, take orders this time and run. Disappear where they'll never find you. You've been bragging that you know how to do that. Prove it."

"But I can't just leave you."

"Andrea, listen to yourself. We're not friends, we're not anything but two people forced into a dangerous situation. I'm heading down."

She stood there, stunned by his awfully cruel words considering the tender stories they'd shared last night. She sat cross-legged on the ground and the dogs sat on either side of her. Watching McKendrick approach the house, she realized he must be pushing her away so they wouldn't get mixed up about their relationship.

Relationship? Is that what you'd call it?

She couldn't deny she felt a connection to him, maybe because he was Jimmy's best friend. She couldn't imagine what it had done to him to spare Jimmy from torture by taking his life. She'd had a dreadful time putting her dog to sleep when he'd been stricken with cancer. She couldn't do it, so Jimmy had taken care of it.

And brought home Daisy to be Oscar's new pal.

Sometimes things have to die to be reborn.

Kyle's words haunted her. Was it possible? Could she be reborn in the light of hope for a happy future? With Kyle?

Whoa, girl. No more mercenaries for you.

Still, she felt as if she was ready to be healed, ready to move on, once she'd escaped the lurking shadow of Biehl.

A few minutes later Kyle stepped onto the front porch with Henry Simpson and waved her down.

She followed the trail to the house. "Henry, hi."

"Andrea, good to see you."

"Kyle told you what's going on?"

"Yes, ma'am. Go ahead and call your brother-in-law. We'll be out here."

"Thanks."

"The house is empty," he said. "Martha and Jill are running errands and the boys are at a rodeo."

"Okay, great." She went inside to the hall phone and put her backpack on a chair. She took a deep, steadying breath and dialed Tom's number. It rang once and a man answered.

"Tom?" she asked.

"No, he's not here."

It couldn't be a Beta Force agent, could it?

"How about Claudia?"

"She's not here either. I'm the neighbor, Chip Edmonds. Who's this?"

"Tom's sister-in-law." She instinctively ducked as if she expected helicopters to swoop down on the house.

"Oh, then you should know they're at the hospital."

"What? Why?"

"There was a car accident. Claudia and A.J. were on their way back from swim class and—"

She hung up, her hand shaking. She was too late. Biehl had gotten to them, her nephew, an innocent little boy. Biehl had hurt him because…because Andrea betrayed him?

"No!" she cried.

"Andrea?"

Kyle came into the house and placed a hand to her shoulder. "What is it?"

"A car accident. A.J. and Claudia…in the hospital."

He pulled her against his chest. The world was spinning out of control and she was unable to stop it.

She pushed away from him. "I want him dead."

"Who?" Henry Simpson said, coming up behind Kyle. "What's going on?"

"Major Biehl. I want him destroyed."

"Don't talk like that," Kyle said.

"That's the only way this will end. Use me as bait if you have to."

"Don't be ridiculous."

"Why? He's after me. Use me to nail the bastard. Tell him I have the evidence."

"That's not an option, Andrea. I will not allow your goodness to be destroyed by vengeance."

"It's too late. My husband's dead, my nephew and his mom are in the hospital and Biehl won't stop until he has what he wants. Tell him I'll meet with him and then…" She paused. "Kill him."

Kyle looked at her with sad brown eyes.

"Do it!" she cried. "Do it or I will. I'll shoot the sonofabitch if you're too much of a coward to kill him."

Years of repressed anguish and festering hatred bubbled up from the depths of her soul, causing the ugly, brutal words to tumble from her mouth. She knew what it felt like to want to destroy something. To kill something.

God, she *had* become one of them.

Frustration burning her throat, she marched outside and leaned against the porch railing. How had it come to this?

"Andrea?"

She closed her eyes at the soft tone of Kyle's voice. Embarrassment flooded her cheeks.

He slipped his arms around her waist from behind. She turned into his embrace and pressed her cheek to his chest. "I hate this feeling," she said. "Angry, hateful and helpless."

"Understandable."

She glanced up at him. "What can I do?"

"I'll take care of it," Kyle said.

"I could find out what hospital they're at," Henry offered, joining them on the porch.

"I don't want to involve you in this," she said.

"But you'd offer yourself as bait," Kyle said.

"I've been hiding behind my denial thinking it would all go away. It won't go away until I make it right."

"I'll contact your brother-in-law," Kyle said. "We need to keep you safe."

"We've got a spare bedroom complete with hiding spot in the floor," Henry proposed. "Previous owners used it to ferment booze."

"Sounds like a good time." Kyle smiled. He was trying to distract her from her pain.

"I can't sit here and do nothing," she said.

"It's not nothing," Kyle offered. "Keeping you safe is the ultimate revenge for Jimmy. And it'll help me stay sane enough to finish this."

"Wait a second, you're leaving?"

"Yes."

She started for the house to grab her backpack, but he placed his hand to her shoulder. "You can't come with me, Andrea."

"What are you talking about?"

"I can't focus if I'm worried about your safety."

"Then don't. I can take care of myself."

"But I can't take care of myself if I'm worried about you being brutalized by the major. Henry has a hiding place where they won't find you. It's perfect because you'll be right under Biehl's nose."

He nodded at Henry. "Why don't you show her the room?"

"I'll do that, then bring you some clothes and supplies."

"Hey, wait a second, I resent being handed off like this," she protested.

Resent it? Face it girl, you're hurt that he's abandoning you.

"Andrea," Kyle said, touching her cheek. "Do you want to destroy Biehl and end this?"

"You know I do."

"Then you need to let me go."

His words touched her heart. "Where?"

"I have some ideas where to look next."

"But—"

"I need to know you're safe. If anything happened to you…"

As she studied his eyes, she sensed he wanted to hold her again, even kiss her, but he held back.

"You'll get through this," he said. "It will be okay, I promise."

For a split second she believed him.

He kissed her on the forehead, a sweet, gentle kiss, then nodded for her to follow Henry. She struggled to keep her emotions in check as she turned away from him.

Grief hovered close again. She was losing this man whom she wished she'd met under different circumstances.

"Andrea?" he said.

She glanced over her shoulder.

"I'll be in touch."

"Thanks." She forced a smile, wanting him to remember her that way.

Oscar trotted alongside her as she followed Henry. She suspected Daisy stayed outside to say good-bye to Kyle.

Andrea couldn't bring herself to say good-bye.

It was best this way. They had no business caring about each other. They were both too damaged.

Henry escorted her to the first-floor bedroom. "We keep the bed made up in case our older boy comes home for a visit. Doesn't happen very often what with his busy career in Denver." He went to the closet and kneeled. "Trap door is here. Plenty of room to hide."

"Thanks."

"My pleasure. I'll let you rest." He closed the door.

She ambled to the window, knowing she wouldn't see Kyle leave from this vantage point. Definitely a good thing. She felt so disassociated from everything, so numb. She glanced at her backpack. She was desperate to make sense of her roller-coaster emotions.

She pulled Jimmy's diary from her backpack and stretched out on the bed. With a deep breath she closed her eyes and rubbed her fingertips across the soft leather. Sadness filled her chest. Not because Jimmy was gone, but because she'd been unable to heal him.

Fighting back the dark memories, exhaustion took hold. It had been two intense days of eluding danger, her emotions racing from one extreme to the other. Kyle was her husband's killer, yet he kept saving her life. Now he was going to warn Tom, but what if Tom didn't believe him? What if he thought Kyle was the enemy?

He *is* the enemy, isn't he?

She must have drifted off because when she opened her eyes it was dark in her room. Slightly disoriented, she switched on the bedside lamp and sat up.

Jimmy's diary slipped to the floor. She'd opened it earlier, but couldn't bring herself to read the words.

She picked it up, flipping through the pages. Her eyes caught on the word *Mac*.

If anything happened to me, I'd want Mac to find Andy and take care of her. They both love me. It's only right that they take care of each other.

"Jimmy?" she whispered, running her fingers over the smooth paper. She flipped a few more pages.

I can't be with her anymore. I've hurt her so badly and I've ruined our relationship. Just like Biehl ruined me. Tommy will know what to do.

Jimmy had contacted Tom about his situation? No, Tom would have said something at the funeral.

Daisy barked outside, drawing her attention to the window. She shoved the diary into her backpack and peeked through the sheers.

Two trucks headed up the Simpson's long driveway. Crouching on the floor, she whistled for Daisy to come and helped her through the window. Thanks to Daisy's protective instincts Beta Force now knew Andrea was here.

She locked the dogs in the bedroom and went into the hallway, calling out for Henry. No answer. She was alone.

A note on the refrigerator caught her eye.

Out checking a sick horse. Martha and Jill will be home at seven with dinner.

She glanced at the stove clock. It was nearly seven now, which meant the Simpson family was walking into an ambush. Martha and Jill, threatened by Beta.

No, this had to stop.

She had to lead the agents away from the farm, had to protect the Simpson family, had to save them.

"Can't panic," she said to herself, adjusting her backpack.

A gunshot chilled her to the bone.

She crouched low and made her way to the living-room window.

A soldier was aiming a rifle at Henry Simpson.

She scrambled to the basement, looking for a firearm, a way to defend herself and Henry. Had to make them leave, had to keep them away and protect Martha and Jill.

They wanted Andrea, so she'd surrender herself.

She found the gun rack, but it was locked. Then she glanced at the workbench and spotted a revolver. She grabbed it, checked to make sure it was loaded, and raced up the stairs.

Without hesitating, she whipped open the front door. "You want me, not him."

"Andy, how good to see you again," Biehl said, his eyes gleaming.

"Let Henry go."

"You lied to us, sir," Biehl said to Henry. "You've been harboring a criminal."

"A criminal?" she said.

"You're an accomplice to McKendrick's treason," Biehl accused.

The soldier took a few steps closer to Henry. She aimed the pistol. "Leave him alone."

"Secure the prisoner," Biehl ordered.

"Henry has nothing to do with this," Andrea argued.

"Private!" Biehl shouted.

The soldier eyed her and took another step toward Henry.

"I said stop!" she cried, and the gun went off.

Two soldiers tackled her and the three of them went down, her head slamming against the hard earth.

Chapter Ten

Andrea heard the rustle of canvas and opened her eyes. She was lying on a cot in a tent, cardboard boxes and sleeping rolls stacked in the corner. She sat up and her stomach lurched.

She squinted to see into the far corner, lit by the soft glow of a lantern. She stood and realized her ankle had been shackled to the cot leg.

"Great." She collapsed on the cot and cradled her head between her hands.

A young soldier popped his head into the tent, then disappeared. "Sir! She's awake," he called.

A minute later Biehl whipped open the tent flap and stepped inside, flanked by two other men. She recognized one of them as Lieutenant Crane.

"Andrea, dear, we were worried about you," Biehl said.

"I'll bet," she said, closing her eyes and rubbing at her forehead.

"We are not the enemy here, and yet you shot Private Lawson, sending him to the hospital."

Regret tore through her. She'd actually hit him? The

last thing she remembered was being slammed to the ground. She wanted to ask how the soldier was, but didn't dare give Biehl the satisfaction.

What about Henry Simpson? She'd never be able to forgive herself if he'd been hurt by these men.

Biehl grabbed a stool and sat beside her. He wore military fatigues and black boots. A pack of cigarettes bulged from his shirt pocket.

"You may go," Biehl said over his shoulder. The younger soldier left.

"I'd like to hear this story if it's all the same to you," Crane said.

Biehl reached over to take her hand.

"Don't touch me." She scooted back on the cot.

"Andy, really. There's no need for that. All I want is your safety. That's why we have to talk. About McKendrick. And maybe, if you help us, I won't file charges for attempted murder." Biehl smiled, that horrible, vicious smile that signaled he was about to strike.

"What happened out there with McKendrick?"

"He's dead." She motioned to Crane. "He killed him."

"Hmmm." Biehl narrowed his eyes. "No, you wouldn't lie to me about McKendrick, the man who dragged Jimmy through hell and back."

"I'm not lying."

"But you ran off with him."

"He took me against my will," she said with as much hatred in her voice as she could muster. Exposing her true feelings for Kyle was Biehl's objective. He'd use it against her, and against Kyle.

Biehl lit a cigarette. "So, you resisted going off with him?"

"Of course I did."

"Rather unfortunate how this all turned out. McKendrick treated Jimmy like a brother at first. The boys had such fun—with their guns, and their women."

She steeled herself against his words.

"McKendrick knew how to seduce his female targets to get information out of them and he shared his secrets with Jimmy."

Her heart beat triple-time. She guessed a man like Kyle would draw women like bees to honey, but knew in her heart he wouldn't encourage Jimmy to be unfaithful to her.

Biehl lifted a finger to his chin and tapped it in contemplation. "I'm so relieved to hear McKendrick is finally dead. I mean, after everything that man did to you and your family."

Biehl sucked on his cigarette and blew smoke at the ceiling. "Poor, poor Jimmy. Your husband worshipped the ground McKendrick walked on. To think McKendrick betrayed Jimmy that way... If it wasn't for McKendrick, well, Jimmy would still be alive today." Biehl shook his head and glanced at the ground.

She was disgusted by his attempted manipulations. She knew the truth, that Biehl had set Jimmy up to die, forcing Kyle to take action.

I couldn't let him die like that.

She clung to Kyle's confession, hoping it would keep her sane during Biehl's interrogation.

Biehl leaned forward. "I need to know what happened out there in the wilderness."

I started to care about one of your cutthroats against my better judgment.

"McKendrick kidnapped me, that's what happened."

"Hmmm. What did the two of you talk about?" Biehl pressed.

Her eyes shot up to meet his. "He killed my husband. What do you think we talked about? He threatened me, and dragged me across the country, and it's your fault for letting him get away!"

"Where were you when my soldiers took him prisoner?"

"Hiding. I was terrified. I didn't know who to trust," she said, her voice trembling. "After all, you'd threatened Jimmy's family."

"My dear, I didn't mean to scare you. I wanted your help and you were being so distrustful and stubborn."

And her nephew was in the hospital.

"Please calm yourself," he said. "It's over now, if you cooperate." His comforting tone nauseated her. It was far from over. She glanced at Biehl's military pins. It would never be over.

"Did McKendrick say anything about having intelligence regarding my unit?"

"No," she lied.

The major smiled and stood. She breathed a sigh of relief.

Suddenly Biehl backhanded her across the cheek and she went face down against the cot. She buried her face into the pillow, fighting the tears brought on by the sting. Oh, how he loved hitting defenseless women. She wondered if he smacked his wife around this way, or just women who were chained and had no way to escape.

"Major?" Crane questioned.

"What?" Biehl snapped back.

Crane remained silent.

Biehl hunkered down next to her and turned her head to face him. "You can help me, or you can die. Your husband had something of mine and McKendrick is determined to find it. You need to help us get it before he does, understand?"

She nodded.

"Keep an eye on her," Biehl ordered Crane, then stormed out of the tent.

Fury bubbled in her chest. If it was the last thing she did, Andrea would destroy Biehl. The man didn't deserve to wear a uniform. Hell, the man didn't deserve to live.

"Andrea?"

She peered out from between her fingers. Lieutenant Crane looked down at her. "I won't hurt you." He put his hands out in a calming gesture.

"I know," she whispered. "Kyle told me about you."

"Do you know where he is?"

She eyed the lieutenant. "No. What happened to Henry Simpson?"

"Nothing. Biehl has no use for him."

"Then he's okay?"

"He's fine, although he wasn't happy about us taking you."

"I...I shot one of your soldiers?"

"A flesh wound. He'll be fine."

She took a deep breath and rubbed her cheek.

"Want a cold pack?" Crane offered.

"I won't give the bastard the satisfaction."

Crane smiled. "Tough girl." His expression turned serious. "Biehl's sending you to a facility outside of Denver. I'm not sure what he plans after that."

She suspected he did, but didn't want to frighten her.

"I'll be right back." He stood and slipped through the tent flap.

Images of her life a week ago raced through her mind, peaceful and pleasant images—planting, brewing, healing.

And now she was chained to a cot, she'd been slapped around, and she'd shot a man.

Crane returned and handed her a cup of water and bottle of aspirin. "The soldier taking you to Denver will have to slow down as he makes his way through Langley Pass. I'm thinking your best bet is to jump from the truck."

"Down a mountainside?"

"I'm not sure you have a choice. I don't know what Biehl's going to do next. I've never seen him like this. McKendrick warned me but I had to see it for myself. That's why I'm here. I've got connections in Washington. I'm going to report back. In the meantime, you need to escape before you reach Denver."

"Okay," she said, cringing at the thought of plummeting down a rocky mountainside.

"Biehl has broken hard-edged soldiers at the base in Denver," he added.

The image of Kyle crying out in his sleep invaded her thoughts.

Crane stood. "Get some sleep."

"My backpack?" she asked.

"Biehl's got it. I'll get it back before you go."

"Thanks."

With a sigh, she curled up, focusing on the best way to jump for her life and not break every bone in her body. Whether she survived or not, at least she'd be away from Biehl.

She shuddered. The man was a monster. As she lay helpless and scared, she realized that each day she was being drawn further into the menacing world of Beta Force. She'd actually shot a soldier, but she'd done so to protect Henry. That was an honorable act, not a heinous one.

Like Kyle killing Jimmy? Her chest tightened. This was so complicated. Yet one thing was very simple: she needed to get away from Biehl before he did unspeakable things to her.

Even if that meant jumping to her death.

MALE VOICES awakened her, not that she was sleeping soundly. She'd been drifting in and out of a state of panic.

"We'll get the truth out of her at The Lab," Biehl said.

"Did you get anything from McKendrick when you had him there?" Crane asked.

Silence, then, "No. The bastard wouldn't break," Biehl said. "But he will."

"How can you be sure?"

"He thinks he killed his best friend, doesn't he?"

"You mean he didn't?" Crane asked.

"He doesn't have the balls." Biehl laughed. "Mind-altering drugs are a wonderful invention, don't you think?"

"When used on the enemy."

She struggled to grasp what they were saying. Kyle hadn't killed Jimmy, but was brainwashed into thinking he had? He beat himself up every day because he thought he'd killed his best friend.

Which is exactly what Biehl wanted: Kyle in a constant state of self-hatred. She had to find him, had to tell him the truth. She had to offer absolution.

Someone pulled the tent flap open. Biehl. She could tell by the cigarette stench.

"Ah, you're awake." He stepped closer. "I wanted to give you another chance to tell us anything you can about McKendrick."

"I don't know anything. I was the victim, remember?"

"Hmmm. No, I don't believe you." He smiled. "Lieutenant Crane, accompany the prisoner to the transport vehicle."

Biehl disappeared and Crane took a few steps forward. He handed her her backpack and removed her ankle cuff. He leaned close. "Did you hear that?" he whispered. "Mac didn't kill Jimmy."

She nodded and he helped her stand.

"Stay alive and away from the Lab," he said in a low voice. They left the tent and the nighttime air chilled her skin as Lieutenant Crane led her to a truck.

"Biehl moves prisoners in the middle of the night," he explained. "He's staying here to continue the search for Mac."

She climbed into the passenger side of an army truck and glanced at the driver. He looked tired. Good. Maybe this would be easier than she thought.

Crane shut the door and they drove off.

Biehl's words set off an inferno in her chest: *Mind-altering drugs are a wonderful invention, don't you think?*

That bastard. He'd gone after everyone she loved, and had mentally destroyed Kyle. She had to get to Kyle and tell him the truth.

The truck groaned its way up a steep road and they passed a sign that read Langley Pass.

She glanced out the window to estimate the drop. Blackness prevented her from seeing more than a few feet beyond the road. How far would she fall if she threw herself into the mercy of the wilderness? The thought wasn't appealing. The thought of Biehl torturing her was worse.

The soldier shifted into low gear as the truck struggled to make it up the incline.

She took a deep breath. *Some things have to die to be reborn.* Kyle's words suddenly made sense. She wasn't afraid anymore. Not of Biehl, or her own grief. For the first time in years, she felt alive, and she was going to fight like hell.

Grabbing her pack, she whipped open the door.

The soldier tugged on her jacket sleeve, but didn't get a good grasp of her arm. She jumped, hit the side of the road and tumbled to the edge...

And over.

Rocks dug into her back and tree limbs clawed at her body, ripping her jacket. She reached out to grab something, anything, to slow the momentum.

"God damn it!" the soldier cried out. Two shots rang out above her.

She struggled to relax against the fall, knowing the more she tensed the more she'd be injured. With a bump she hit a plateau. Cold, wet earth soaked through her jacket and shirt, chilling her skin.

She opened her eyes and stared into the star-filled sky. Then a flickering light sent adrenaline coursing through her. Her captor was coming down after her. She scrambled to her feet, put on her backpack and took off, thanking God she hadn't broken anything in the fall.

Gasping for breath, she raced through the trees to put as much distance as possible between herself and Biehl's soldier.

A man's voice called out, but she didn't turn around. She knew who was behind her. Would he shoot her in the back as she ran away?

Faster. Had to run faster.

Fear drove her down the trail at a frantic speed. She wasn't even sure which direction she ran in. It didn't matter, as long as it was away from the truck.

The crunch of footsteps closed in and panic sent her into a desperate sprint. She couldn't lose like this. Hadn't Biehl taken enough of her life?

"No," she muttered through jagged breaths.

She had to make it, had to tell Kyle he wasn't a killer, he hadn't killed Jimmy.

Grabbed from behind, she swung wildly at her assailant.

"Andrea! Stop!"

Her breath caught at the sound of Kyle's voice. Her eyes shot open and she didn't know if she should laugh or cry. "Kyle?"

"You should have been a boxer," he said, squinting.

"But I thought…Biehl's soldier—"

He started up the trail, pulling her behind him. "We've gotta move."

"Wait, you need to know, I've got to tell you—"

He turned suddenly. And kissed her.

WHITE LIGHTNING shot across Kyle's nerve endings, making him dizzy and short of breath. He expected Andrea to fight him, maybe throw another punch.

Instead her tongue darted out to tickle his lips and he broke apart. He couldn't help himself. She was safe and alive, and relief clouded his better judgment. Somehow he'd known it would be like this: pure and all-consuming.

But he had no business kissing her. He broke the kiss and held her by the shoulders. "I'm sorry, that was wrong."

He led her deeper into the woods. He couldn't look at her or speak to her, thanks to the emotional knot lodged in his chest. He'd almost lost her. His blood pressure jumped at the thought of Andrea being imprisoned at The Lab.

The warmth of her hand shot up his arm. He was losing his edge because he feared for her life, but this is all part of war. Things happen, people get hurt, loved ones die.

Not Andrea. He wouldn't let anything happen to Andrea.

He headed for the ranch he'd spotted earlier when planning her rescue. Thanks to Crane's radio he knew where Biehl's men were. He'd heard them talk about her capture. He knew Biehl would most likely move her in the middle of the night, and Kyle was ready.

"Over there," Kyle whispered, crouching down in the brush. "That ranch. See the truck? I'm going to hot-wire it." He turned, and studied her face. Dirt smudged her forehead, her right cheek was swollen and her jacket was torn.

He reached out and touched her cheek. He couldn't say it in words, couldn't explain how sorry he was that she'd been abducted by Biehl.

She leaned forward and kissed him. He fought it at first, then gave in, couldn't resist deepening the kiss that burned a trail straight to his heart.

A heart that had opened up to this woman.

Remembering where they were, he pulled away and traced his finger along her hairline. "When you hear me start the truck, meet me by the road."

"Okay." She looked tired and beaten, nothing like the bold woman he'd first discovered at the cabin. He couldn't help but blame himself. How could he have left her?

Because he thought she'd be safer with the Simpsons.

No, Mac. You left because you were terrified of falling in love with her.

He could no longer deny the truth. He shoved it back and focused on getting her safe.

He approached the dark and quiet house. Kyle opened the truck door and released the parking brake. He put the truck in Neutral, and, with one hand on the wheel, pushed it away from the house. A safe distance away, he cut and touched the necessary wires with a knife he'd taken off Biehl's soldier. The engine turned over and he steered the truck toward the road, but didn't see Andrea.

"Where are you?" he whispered, frantically scanning the area. Impatient, he stopped the truck and got out.

"I'm here, I'm here," she said, limping toward him. "I don't move as fast as I used to." She climbed into the front seat, pain creasing her forehead.

He wanted to kick himself for not being more sensitive to her injuries. She'd fallen down a mountainside and that wasn't the worst of it. What had Biehl done to her? He shoved the truck in gear and headed down the two-lane highway.

"Where are we going?"

"Colorado Springs." He glanced at her. "You need to talk to Jimmy's brother, don't you?"

She nodded.

"That's where we're going."

"Kyle?"

"Yes, ma'am?"

"You didn't kill Jimmy."

Chapter Eleven

His fingers tightened around the steering wheel as hope arced through his chest. How he wished it were true.

"What are you talking about, Andrea? I was there, I remember."

"You remember what they want you to remember. I overheard Biehl talking to Crane."

"I remember shooting him."

"No, it was the drugs."

"I know what I did. It was real." He knew, deep in his gut, that he was responsible for his friend's death and nothing would change that.

"Why won't you believe me?" she said.

"Because I don't want to be manipulated again by Biehl. I killed Jimmy. I didn't kill Jimmy. Back and forth, back and forth. I know what I did."

She folded her arms across her chest and glanced out the window. How could he explain it to her? How could he admit that if he didn't kill Jimmy there was nothing to prevent him from kissing her again, holding her.

Making love to her.

It can never happen, Mac. She deserves better.
Andrea was meant to have a storybook life complete
with caring husband, kids and a cabin in the mountains.
All the things Kyle did not deserve.

Maybe, just maybe, if he finished this thing for his
friend and put Biehl away, Kyle could live a peaceful
life. Alone. But he'd never deserve the woman sitting
next to him. His best friend's wife. Jimmy had been her
true love. She could never love another man that way,
definitely not Kyle. He knew how she despised what he
did for the Force.

Truth was, he'd caught himself fantasizing about
settling down, opening an adventure sports shop somewhere in a mountain town. He'd saved enough money.

What the hell was he doing thinking about the future?

"I thought you were long gone," she said. She still
refused to look at him.

"I heard about your capture on the radio and caught
up with Biehl. Found his camp and was waiting for the
right time to rescue you."

She nodded.

"He didn't hurt you, did he?"

"No, just a slap." She waved her hand.

He ground his teeth. He wanted to rip the guy's
eyeballs out.

"He asked a lot of questions. Talked about you and
Jimmy—and women," she said.

"You didn't believe him?"

"No, not about Jimmy. I don't think he'd be unfaithful to me."

Which meant she did believe whatever lies Biehl

had told about Kyle. Good, those would keep her away. Maybe she'd slap him the next time he lost it and kissed her.

"We'll get close to your brother-in-law's and call. Going to the house is out of the question. I'm sure Biehl's watching it."

"Whatever you think is best." She was being too agreeable.

"You okay?"

"Sure, fine." Like hell she was.

THEY DROVE the next few hours in silence, Kyle listening to the radio Crane had given him, and Andrea trying to figure out why he didn't embrace his newfound innocence. She'd told him that he hadn't killed Jimmy, yet he wouldn't believe her. Why was he holding onto the guilt?

"There." He pointed to a small motel along the side of the road. "I'll drop you off. Register under a false name and I'll ditch the car and meet you there. Try and get that end room."

"Are you sure we should stop?"

"Sure. We'll call your brother from the room and get you cleaned up before you go visit him. If you go like that you'll freak him out."

Right. She must look like hell. She started to flip down the visor to look in the mirror but he placed his hand to hers.

"Don't," he said. "You look fine."

Something in his voice warmed her heart.

"What about Biehl?"

"He's camped a good twenty miles away." He motioned to his radio. "I've been listening." He pulled into the parking lot and she reached for the door.

"Wait," he said. "Let's wipe the smudges off your face."

She leaned forward and he rubbed his shirt cuff against her forehead, then her jaw. She couldn't help but appreciate the concern in his warm brown eyes.

Genuine concern.

He caught her staring at him and he froze. "You're really okay?"

"Yes." She was, as long as he was close.

He leaned forward and kissed her, and the moan that escaped her throat surprised her. She placed her hand against his chest for support, for reassurance that he was still here, protecting her from the horrors of the last few days.

He broke the kiss and she struggled to clear her thoughts. She noticed he was breathing heavily.

"Go on," he said, reaching over and opening the door.

She got out of the truck and went to the motel office.

Minutes later she was registered as Samantha Trendell. The manager didn't ask for identification, not after she flashed two fifty-dollar bills in his face for a sixty-dollar room. Andrea always kept an emergency stash in her pack.

She flipped the motel-room light on. Vintage seventies wood paneling stretched from one end of the room to the other. She stripped off her jacket, flopped on the bed and stared at the ceiling. It all felt so surreal, especially Kyle's kisses.

She wanted more of them.

She went to the window and peered outside. It seemed like hours since he'd dropped her off.

Worry filled her chest. No, she'd think positively. They'd come so far and she was so close to calling Tom and finally warning him. She hoped he'd believe her.

She picked up the phone and called her brother-in-law. The answering machine picked up. A soft knock made her jump. She hung up, grabbed the lamp from the nightstand and went to the door.

"Andrea? It's me," Kyle whispered.

Relieved, she sighed and unlocked the door. A ragged Kyle McKendrick walked in and locked the door behind him. He glanced at her weapon of choice and raised a brow.

"I'm prepared," she said.

"I'm glad."

She put the lamp on the nightstand. "What took you so long?"

"Ditching the truck was a little tougher than I thought." He stripped off his sweatshirt.

Good grief, if he kept stripping all the way down to his birthday suit, she was sunk.

Why? It's not wrong to be attracted to this man.

Uh, he's a mercenary, remember?

Who wants out of the business.

"Anybody home?" he said, smiling at her.

"Sorry, I was having an argument with myself."

"Did you win?"

"Very funny. What can I do for you?" she said, then blushed at the innuendo. "To help find the evidence against Biehl."

He pulled her into his arms, stroking her hair. "In good time. First let's contact your brother-in-law."

They stood there for a few minutes, holding each

other. For the first time in years, she felt grounded, at peace.

"You want to wash up?" he said.

"I smell that bad, huh?"

"No, I meant—"

"I'm kidding." She placed a quick kiss to his lips and swiped an oversized T-shirt from her backpack.

"I called Tom. No answer."

"We'll try again tomorrow."

She nodded and went into the bathroom. She was giving him space for now, but he wasn't going to avoid dealing with the fact that something had developed between them. For the first time in a long time, she wasn't going to run away. Not from Kyle or from the way she felt about him.

Twenty minutes later she'd showered and slipped on the T-shirt. She opened the bathroom door. The last thing she expected to find was an unconscious warrior sprawled on his back, a TV remote dangling from his fingertips. Other than the soft glow of the television, the room was dark and peaceful. She sat next to Kyle on the bed and stroked his cheek.

An impossible situation. That's what they were in right now. Running from the enemy, not knowing who to trust, falling helplessly in love. She couldn't deny it. She was falling for Kyle McKendrick.

Studying his angular features, she brushed her fingertips along the soft planes of his mouth. She knew how badly he needed absolution. She had a feeling it was more important to Kyle than anything, maybe even love.

She peeked beneath the gauze to examine his wound,

which was healing better than she'd expected. She stretched out next to him and placed a hand on his naked chest.

He opened his eyes and blinked.

"I didn't mean to wake you," she said.

He shifted onto his side and looked into her eyes. "I'm sorry I left you at the Simpsons'. I shouldn't have done that."

"Shhh." She pressed her fingers to his lips. "How could you know they'd find me?"

"Why didn't you hide in the floorboards?"

"They'd seen Daisy outside, they knew I was there. I didn't want them punishing Henry."

"You're always putting everyone else first."

"It's who I am."

He smiled.

"Kiss me again?" She'd surprised herself with the request.

"We shouldn't." He glanced at his hand as he fingered her hair.

"Why?"

"This isn't real, Andrea. After we nail Biehl, we'll go our separate ways."

"Jimmy wished for us to be together."

His gaze snapped up to meet hers.

"He wrote as much in his journal," she said. "He wrote about us finding each other, taking care of each other if anything ever happened to him."

"No, he was my best friend and I—I won't betray him again."

"You didn't kill him. Why can't you believe that?"

He rolled onto his back and stared at the ceiling. "It doesn't matter if I pulled the trigger. I'm responsible for getting him involved in Beta Force, you said so yourself."

"Stop hiding behind your guilt."

He turned to her, fire in his eyes. "Is that what I'm doing?"

"Look, Jimmy's gone. I've let go of that part of my life. Don't let him come between us."

"He'll never be anywhere else."

"I disagree." She pulled him close and kissed him.

KYLE COULD'VE kept it together as long as Andrea didn't touch him.

Then she kissed him and it was all over. She was an enchantress drawing him into her spell. When he kissed her back the connection set him on fire from his lips down to other places that ached for her love. Need consumed him as the kiss deepened and her hands roamed his back. Her moan of surrender made him want to strip off her shirt. Common sense slapped him back to reality.

He pushed away from her. "Andrea, are you sure?"

"Absolutely." She smiled and his chest tightened. Her expression said it all. She trusted Kyle with her heart.

He found himself forgetting all of his sins, the lies. He needed her here, beside him, for as long as he could keep her.

He kissed her, seductively, but gently, because he wanted this night to be the one she'd remember for the rest of her life. Kyle wanted her to know he could be tender and giving. He needed her to know how much he cared.

He stripped off her shirt. She was naked underneath,

and he wondered if she'd known they'd make love, if she wanted it to happen as much as he did. Her eyes drifted shut, and he laid a sweet and gentle kiss on her lips. His hand explored the soft skin of her belly and slowly edged up to cup her breast. His fingers grazed the sensitive peak and her moan sent a shiver down his back.

He needed to be inside her, now and forever. Her fingers threaded through his hair as she pulled his mouth to her breast. When she arched and cried out he thought he'd completely lose it.

But he couldn't. He'd promised himself that if he ever held her in his arms, he'd pleasure her in ways she'd never imagined. Slow, seductive ways. Magical, tender ways.

And here she was, the length of her body pressed against his, writhing, wanting something that only he could give. He slid his hand to cup her backside, her silken skin so perfect against him, warming his entire body with its heat.

"Kyle," she whispered.

He caressed the fair skin of her shoulders and down, tracing her ribs with his fingers. She gripped his shoulders as if she feared falling off a cliff. But he wouldn't let her go, not until he was ready to fall with her.

As his fingers touched the magical spot between her legs, she cried out, her voice bordering on frustration. "Kyle…please," she said, her eyes squeezed shut, her breathing labored.

This was her night. He'd give her whatever she wanted, whenever she wanted it. He shucked his pants and pressed against her, their bodies entwined, his heart pounding with need. She clung to him, pulled him closer, and he feared he'd crush her with his weight. Her fingernails dug into his back as she opened for him. He marveled at her complete abandon.

To him.

He couldn't pull away now if both their lives depended on it. His mouth was warm and hot on hers as he surrendered, losing himself to the beauty and the magic. Somewhere in the recesses of his mind a voice whispered that this time, in Andrea's arms, he had relinquished a part of his soul.

Chapter Twelve

Andrea awakened sated and content. Kyle's arm was flung protectively across her body from behind. It couldn't get much better than this, she thought. His fingers grazed her breast.

"Hmmm," she sighed. "Again?"

"We should get going. And I need a shower."

She rolled over to face him, stroking the soft hairs on his chest.

"You'd better stop or we're never getting out of this hotel room," he said.

"Sorry." She smiled, but she wasn't sorry.

He slid a strand of hair behind her ear. "I've been thinking."

She hoped it was about their future. How did one date a wounded, retired mercenary? "About what?" she asked.

"We both know Jimmy was volatile in the end, but he also was determined."

So much for him dreaming about their life together.

"I'm wondering if he sent the evidence against Biehl someplace safe. Safe, but obvious," he said.

"Like, to his brother?"

"It's possible." He sighed. "I'm grasping at straws, I know. I want this to be over."

She pushed him onto his back and kissed him. God, she would never get used to the way his lips tasted. She broke the kiss. "As a good friend once said to me, have faith."

He pressed his forehead against hers, his breathing short and labored. She loved that she affected him this way.

"You're amazing," he said.

"Really?" She leaned back and winked.

"Don't start."

"I know, we've got to get moving. Go take your shower."

He narrowed his eyes, then claimed her with a sizzling kiss. His lips felt so incredibly right. So perfect.

When he broke the contact she could have sworn his lips trembled. He got out of bed, completely uninhibited by his nakedness, and grabbed his clothes from the floor. She studied his muscular backside and smiled with satisfaction. This courageous, sexy man was hers. She didn't know for how long, but for now they were together.

"Behave," he ordered, disappearing into the bathroom.

She flopped against the starched sheets and sighed, remembering their tender, yet passionate lovemaking. It was as if she and Kyle were meant to find each other at this tumultuous time in their lives. How was that possible?

She smiled to herself and slipped out of bed. As she started to dress, she heard the shower go on. It was so tempting to climb in with Kyle and wash his back, his arms, his...

"Then we'll never get out of here," she muttered,

plucking her socks from the floor. She considered what she'd say when she contacted her brother-in-law. Would Tom even speak to her after the way she'd abandoned the family? How could she convince him that the car accident had been caused by Biehl?

Her stomach twisted into a knot. Her sweet little nephew had been hurt thanks to Jimmy's involvement with Beta Force. The ugly story would have to come out, but not over the phone. It would be too easy for Tom to hang up, to deny his little brother's culpability. She had to look into Tom's eyes when she told him this one. She might even have to describe Jimmy's violent ways. Her chest ached at the thought. She'd have to unearth the grief she'd buried to maintain her sanity.

Sitting on the edge of the bed, she reached for the phone and hesitated. She dreaded hearing about her injured nephew and his mom. She felt responsible.

She snatched her hand back and took a deep breath.

"What's wrong?" Kyle asked from the bathroom doorway.

She glanced over her shoulder. He stood there with a towel around his waist, drying his hair with a second towel. "I'm afraid to call my brother-in-law."

"Afraid of what?" He sat beside her on the bed.

"Should I make a list? Let's see, that he hates me, that he won't believe me." She paused and looked into his eyes. "That my nephew was seriously hurt and it's my fault."

"Hey." He cradled her cheeks with his hands. "You know that's not true."

She stood and paced to the window. "I should have gotten to Tom sooner and warned him."

"Look, we don't even know if Biehl caused the accident."

She shot him a look of disbelief.

"We don't." He came up behind her and placed his arm around her shoulder. "But we need to be smart about this. You need to talk to Tom without Biehl finding out. Can you think of a place that would have special significance to the two of you?"

"Jimmy, Tom and I went to the Garden of the Gods once. Huge red rocks sprout up from the ground, it's amazing. Anyway, we got a picture of Jimmy pushing on a rock that looked like it was going to crash down on Tom. We joked about it. Jimmy was Wile E. Coyote and Tom was Road Runner. Get it? The Coyote was trying to push the rock on top of Road Runner. If I could get him out there…"

"Make sure you tell him to come alone."

She nodded and reached for the phone again. "What if they trace it?"

"They can't if you get off quick enough. Tell him to meet you around," he checked the clock, "three this afternoon."

She had the operator place the call. Her pulse raced, her hands started to sweat.

"Hello?"

"Tom?"

"No, hang on."

She glanced at Kyle and he nodded with encouragement.

"Hello?"

"Tom, it's Andrea."

Silence.

"Where are you?" he asked.

"I need to see you. Remember when Wile E. Coyote tipped the boulder on Road Runner? Don't say it out loud. Do you remember?" she pushed, trying to keep the panic from her voice.

"I remember."

"I'll meet you there at three. Make sure you're not followed."

"Not followed? What the hell's going on? I haven't heard from you in years and now—"

"Come alone. It's important." She gripped the receiver. "How is A.J.?"

"Fine, we're all fine. Now tell me—"

The line went dead. Kyle had hung up.

Andrea nodded, sadness filling her chest. "It's all set. He'll meet us at Garden of the Gods."

"Good." He started to get dressed.

"And then?"

"And then what?"

"What will you do after we meet with Jimmy's brother?"

He ripped his gaze from hers. "Our goal is to stay alive for another day. We'll worry about tomorrow when tomorrow comes."

He kissed her, and it felt suspiciously like good-bye.

THEY SCANNED the powerful rocks sprouting up from the ground at the National park. "They're like sculptures," Kyle said, walking along the trail.

Andrea enjoyed the awed expression on his face.

They were careful to avoid large groups of people. Kyle had bought hats and sweatshirts at a tourist stand on the side of the road. She'd twisted her long hair into a bun and tucked it into her hat.

"Incredible, isn't it?" she said.

"Indescribable." He took her hand and she smiled to herself. It was an unconscious gesture on his part. He cared about her.

The sun cast dark shadows as it hit the protruding rocks. She knew their lives weren't simple and that once this was over she'd probably have to start fresh somewhere—by herself. She shivered.

"You look cold." He put his arm around her and they found a spot to hide near the meeting point. Closing her eyes, she leaned into his chest. Oh yeah, she could definitely get used to this.

"Andrea?" he whispered. "It's nearly three. Are you ready?"

"I guess."

He cupped her chin between his thumb and forefinger and tipped her face. "Tell him the truth, even if it hurts."

A few minutes later she spied a man walking up the trail toward them. The man hesitated by the tipping rock, placed his hand on the stone and bowed his head as if in prayer.

"It's Tom," she whispered.

"Go on," Kyle urged.

She slid out of her hiding spot and walked quietly toward her brother-in-law. She'd know from his immediate reaction if he welcomed her presence or resented it.

"Tom?" she said.

He spun around and squinted. "Andrea? It really is you. We thought, we were told…"

"What?"

"It doesn't matter. You're here." Her burly, red-headed brother-in-law gave her a hug.

He broke the embrace and stepped back. "God, kid, it's good to see you."

"You too, Tommy. I'm sorry it had to be so cloak-and-dagger. I've got a lot to tell you."

"We've been so worried."

She warmed at his concern. "You still care."

"Of course I care. You're family."

"I've missed you guys."

"You don't have to miss us. Come home with me."

She looked into his eyes. "Tommy, there are some bad people after me. I don't want to bring that kind of danger to your home."

"It's about Jimmy, isn't it?"

"What makes you say that?"

"His superior officer called the house and said you're in trouble. What happened, honey? What's going on?"

"That superior officer, Major Biehl? He'll kill me if he catches me."

"What?" He took a step back. "That makes no sense."

"It's true, and it's complicated."

"Come home and explain it to me. I want to help. That's all I ever wanted, is to help you and my baby brother."

She recognized the sparkle in his eye, the love that she hadn't felt for years since her split with the family.

"That's not a good idea," she said.

"Nonsense."

"Biehl might be responsible for A.J.'s accident."

"What!" Tom's face lit red with anger.

"He threatened to hurt A.J. if I didn't help him track down one of his missing agents. I called your house to warn you and that's how I found out about the accident. It all adds up."

"No, some teenager wasn't paying attention and side-swiped Claudia, that's all. They went to the hospital as a precaution. They're both fine. Now, come home with me. I want to hear all of this." Tom put his arm around Andrea to lead her away.

"I'm afraid she can't do that." Kyle stepped out from behind the rock.

"Who the hell are you?"

"I'm Kyle McKendrick. A friend of Andrea, and of Jimmy." He extended his hand.

Tom eyed Kyle for a minute before shaking his hand. "Tom Franks."

They shook hands in restrained politeness. Something flared in Tom's eyes. He always had been over-protective of his younger siblings; Andrea felt honored she still fell into that category.

"Kyle saved my life more times than I can count these last couple of days," she explained.

"Really?" Tom asked, disbelief in his voice.

"Kyle and Jimmy were in the service together," she said. "But then they got involved in something else. It's…a long story."

"I've got time," Tom said, eyeing Kyle.

"We belonged to a mercenary group called Beta

Force. Our commanding officer, Major Biehl, recruited us for special assignments."

"This is news to me." Tom turned to her. "Did you know about this mercenary business?"

"Not until after Jimmy died."

"You didn't tell us."

"I didn't want to spoil your memories of him. Tom, Jimmy did some bad things."

"Like what?"

"He killed people, blew things up, other things…"

Things to me, her heart cried out. She couldn't say the words.

"Beta Force brainwashes young soldiers and turns them into killing machines," Kyle said. "He wasn't responsible for some of the things he did."

"My brother was an intelligent man," Tom argued.

"He was a trusting person," she said. "And he wanted his big brother's respect so much."

"So much that he'd become a killer? No, I don't buy it."

"That's your choice," Kyle said. "But I've got to stop Biehl before more soldiers are turned into killers against their will."

Eyes trained on Kyle, Tom asked, "And how do they train you to kill against your will?"

"They threaten your family."

Tom glanced at Andrea and she nodded her confirmation.

"Biehl is trying to find evidence Jimmy stole," Kyle explained. "It would destroy Biehl and his army."

"Correct me if I'm wrong, but you belong to that army."

"I did. I left. My punishment will be death, if he finds me."

"Tom." She touched his arm. "You need to understand the gravity of this situation."

"So, what are you going to do now?"

She glanced at Kyle and back at Tom. "Keep running, I guess, until we find the evidence against Biehl."

"At least stop by the house and see the kids," Tom said. "Just for a second."

"They're probably watching the house," Kyle said.

"Don't be paranoid. They're not after us. The car accident was an accident, no one caused that." He searched Andrea's eyes. "You've gotta see A.J. He looks a lot like Jimmy did at his age. And Katy Ann is nearly six. She's a beauty. Please, Andrea. Come home with me."

"I REALLY CAN'T." She glanced at Kyle and his breath caught at the yearning in her eyes. When she looked at him like that he'd promise her anything.

"If we're careful," Kyle offered.

"Kyle? Are you sure?"

"I've been listening in on their frequency. They're still west of us. A quick visit should be okay."

She threw her arms around his neck. He couldn't ignore Tom's disapproving glare. He clearly wasn't pleased with Andrea's new relationship and Kyle couldn't blame him.

Kyle devised a plan for them to sneak into the house without being seen. Tom dropped Andrea and Kyle four blocks away and drove around to make sure he wasn't being followed.

They hid in the trees near the house until Tom gave them the signal. Tom and Kyle searched the first floor for listening devices and found only one, in the kitchen.

"There could be more," Kyle said.

"Then we'll talk real soft." Tom glared and called for his wife.

She came downstairs and her face lit when she saw Andrea. "My God! Andrea?" The women embraced. "Tom always said you'd come around." She glanced at Kyle. "Hello?"

"This is Kyle McKendrick," Andrea said. "A friend of Jimmy's."

"Nice to meet you." Claudia shook Kyle's hand.

Andrea glanced down at her blond-haired niece, Katy Ann, who clung to Claudia's pant leg.

"Katy Ann, you remember your Auntie Andy, don't you?"

The little girl shifted behind her mother. "Give her time, she'll warm up," Claudia said, cheerfully leading them into the kitchen. Tom closed the blinds and drapes.

"Where's A.J.?" Andrea asked.

"He was right behind me," Claudia said, looking over her shoulder. "A.J.? Honey? Where are you?"

Andrea's heart skipped a beat and the walls closed in. Kyle and Tom must have read her thoughts because the three of them tore through the house calling A.J.'s name.

Chapter Thirteen

"It's okay, sweetheart. I'm sure he's here," Kyle said.

Nothing would calm Andrea except the face of the innocent child she'd come to protect. She whipped open a closet door and Kyle checked under a bed. They met up with Tom in the upstairs hallway.

"Basement," Tom said, and the three of them trampled downstairs.

"You know I never let the baby go into that filthy basement. What's with you guys?" Claudia said.

They scrambled from corner to corner of the musty basement. Nothing. The pounding of Andrea's heart reverberated in her ears. "He's okay, he's okay," she muttered, opening the crawl space door and peering inside.

"Anything?" Tom called.

"No," Kyle answered.

"Excuse me. Hello down there," Claudia said from the basement door.

Andrea ran to the foot of the stairs and looked at her sister-in-law.

"You might want to check his favorite hiding places before tearing apart the basement."

"Where?" Andrea asked.

"The bathroom, kitchen cabinets, behind the couch—"

She raced up the stairs. "Bathroom?"

"Down the hall. He's got a thing about shower stalls," Claudia offered.

Andrea pushed open the bathroom door and took a deep breath to calm herself. Then she heard it. The murmurs of a child immersed in fantasy. She opened the shower door. Big blue eyes stared back at her. She crouched down to A.J.'s level.

"Tack! Tack!" A.J. cried, shoving a plastic action figure at her.

"Hi there," she said, her voice hoarse with emotion.

A.J. mumbled something indiscernible, looked at her and smiled. Jimmy's smile. Jimmy's clear blue eyes. Would her child have looked like this? An angelic face framed by blond curly hair? Would his cheeks have dimpled when he grinned?

"See, see, Mama." The little boy stood, clutching an action figure in each hand.

"A.J.? Could I have a hug?" Andrea asked.

He hesitated, tipped his head to one side, then leaned into her. She closed her eyes and held him, trying not to scare the boy by squeezing too tightly. Baby-smell assailed her senses, a mixture of powder and mild laundry detergent.

"Hey, you should be honored," Claudia said from the doorway. "Two-year-olds aren't keen on strangers."

"Mama, see, see!" A.J. cried, then pushed away from Andrea and went to his mother.

"Mama sees, A.J."

Andrea swiped tears from her face and smiled at the mother and child. Tom and Kyle stood behind Claudia.

"Andrea, what is it?" Claudia said, picking up A.J. and adjusting him to her hip.

"She'll be okay," Kyle said, edging his way into the bathroom. "We'll be out in a minute." He closed the door and sat down, wrapping his arms around her.

"I thought..." she started.

"I know, sweetheart. It's okay. He's okay." The strength of his arms slowly dissolved the horror of the last few minutes.

"I thought he was gone and it was my fault."

"Shhh. He's fine."

"What if Biehl had kidnapped him?"

"He didn't." He looked into her eyes. "The boy's okay. You're okay."

"Not really." It ripped her apart to think what could have happened.

Someone knocked on the door. "Claudia's making spaghetti, can you stay?" Tom said.

Andrea couldn't speak.

"For a few minutes," Kyle answered. "We could use something to go."

"Come out when you're ready."

She sighed. "A.J.'s adorable, isn't he?"

"Yep. Reminds me of Jimmy."

They sat there for a few minutes. Precious minutes she was losing with her niece and nephew. "Let's get out there and enjoy the time we have."

He helped her up and she splashed water on her face. "Okay, almost human," she whispered into the mirror.

She turned and he planted a kiss on her lips. "Better than human." He smiled.

With a kiss and a smile, Kyle McKendrick was able to bring her out of her funk. She felt hope for the first time in years.

They headed into the kitchen where Claudia was making dinner. A.J. raced a truck across the linoleum floor, and Katy was coloring in her Precious Princess book.

"Andrea, why don't you play with the kids while I make sandwiches for you guys?" Claudia suggested.

"Sure, okay."

"I've got supplies downstairs you might want to take with you," Tom said. "Kyle, you want to help me bring them up?"

"Sure." He smiled at Andrea, but didn't kiss her.

They went into the basement and Andrea sat on the kitchen floor out of Claudia's way. "So, Miss Katy, what's your favorite toy?" she asked.

The little girl giggled and Andrea ached for something she'd never have. She could never live a normal, suburban life with Kyle.

But that didn't make her stop wanting it.

"SHUT THE DOOR, will you?" Tom asked.

Kyle hesitated before he pulled it closed, enjoying the sounds of a mother and her children cooking and playing in the kitchen.

Family. Had Kyle's family ever been this happy? He couldn't remember his early days, only the teen years fraught with guilt and responsibility that a kid his age shouldn't have had to deal with.

The smell of sweet tobacco assaulted his nostrils as he stepped onto the cement floor. His gaze drifted around the room to a display case of handguns, rifles and a shotgun. He ran his fingertips across the glass door.

So much death. He seemed chained to it.

"Pretty nice, huh?" Tom asked, lighting a pipe.

"You've got some fine pieces here." He studied a Winchester rifle.

"Yep, I've been collecting guns for years. This one's my favorite."

Kyle turned and found himself staring down the barrel of a Colt .45.

"Tom?" He automatically raised his hands.

"Sit down on the floor, next to the support beam." Tom motioned with the gun.

He went to the metal beam, his mind ticking off his options. He had none. If he charged Tom, somebody could be shot. He thought about the women and kids upstairs. No one would be shot tonight, not in this loving home.

Resisting would only cause more heartache. Tom's actions had to be born of fear, not anger. Tom had no reason to want to hurt Kyle. He just didn't trust him.

Kyle sat down.

"Here." Tom tossed handcuffs at him. "Cuff yourself to the beam."

He did as ordered, then looked up at Tom.

"The major is coming back for you tonight."

"Sonofabitch, Tom, listen to me." He pulled on the cuffs. "He'll kill you and your family."

"He told me you killed Jimmy!"

"No, that's not true." And for the first time since

Jimmy's death Kyle didn't feel guilty for that atrocity. He was starting to forgive himself, thanks to Andrea.

"You're lying," Tom said. "I can see it in your eyes."

"What you see is my guilt for involving Jimmy in Beta Force. He was a good kid and deserved better."

"Damn straight." Tom paced the basement. "Who the hell do I believe?"

"Not Biehl."

"He was Jimmy's superior officer."

"Who has turned into a power-hungry bastard. He's out of his mind. Listen to me, Tom, I was Jimmy's best friend in the Force. He was trying to destroy Biehl."

"Biehl said you raped Andrea."

Anger coursed through him. "Does she act like I raped her? Biehl will say anything to find us. He's in a panic and wants to get the evidence that Jimmy stole, then bury all the loose ends. Me and Andrea, we're loose ends."

"Jimmy was a good kid."

"Yes, he was."

Tom sat down in a beat-up sliding rocker.

"He was a good kid and he admired his big brother," Kyle said. "He talked about going to the Dunes when you were kids. How you used to have races from the top."

Tom eyed him and Kyle thought he might be getting through. Instead, Tom stood and dug into a tool box. Great, was he going to torture Kyle?

He disappeared behind the stairs.

"Tom?" Kyle said.

He came into sight with a metal box. He kneeled beside Kyle and opened it. "I saw what my brother did to people. This was sent to him, here, after his death." He opened an envelope and spilled photographs on the floor.

"Damn. Smart kid," Kyle muttered.

"Smart? You call this smart?"

"Jimmy sent this. It's the evidence we need to have Biehl court-marshaled. We can finally stop the bastard."

"How?"

"I'll take it to someone higher up the chain of command. To Biehl's superior officer."

"It will all come out, won't it? I mean, Jimmy's part in this?"

"Not necessarily. I have a feeling they won't want to make this public. They'll take care of Biehl in their own way."

"Why should I believe you?"

"We're in a mess and I'm partly to blame. I'd like to end this and make sure Andrea is safe—for the rest of her life."

"What, with you?" Tom glared.

"No. But I need to destroy Biehl in order to keep her safe."

Tom stared at the photographs.

"Tom, your brother admired you for always doing the right thing. He mentioned the time he was messing around with a gun and hit the neighbor's dog by accident. He was so ashamed, but you made him own up to his mistake."

Tom's gaze shot. "He never told anyone that story. He was too ashamed."

"We were good friends. He died trying to save everyone else. Please let me make this right for him, and for Andrea."

Tom cocked his head in question. "You're involved with her?"

Kyle evaded Tom's question. "Look, she deserves better than this hell, but she's confused right now and maybe even thinks she loves me."

Tom's eyes widened.

"It's just the intensity of the situation," Kyle explained. "In a few months she'll forget all about me."

His chest ached with the admission.

"It's so damned confusing," Tom said.

"Let me finish what your brother started," Kyle said. "He was trying to destroy an evil man who uses the military as a shield. Jimmy really was the hero."

Tom took a drag off his pipe, blew out the smoke and shook his head.

"Now it's your turn," Kyle said. "I need you to get Andrea away from here and keep her safe, at least until I can nail Biehl."

"She'll want to go with you. I've seen that look in her eyes before." He hesitated. "When she dated my brother."

"I'll take care of it. Promise me not to let her out of your sight."

Tom uncuffed Kyle. "For Jimmy," he whispered.

"For Jimmy."

Tom grabbed a backpack from beneath his workbench and handed it to him. "You can take this for food, a change of clothes. I've got something that'll fit."

"Thanks."

"What are you going to tell her?"

He slid the photographs into the backpack. "That she's safer away from me. That we shared intense emotions born of danger, not love."

"Is that the truth?" Tom asked.

"More or less." He waved Tom off. "How will you keep her safe? I need to know. I left her once before and Biehl got her."

"Don't worry. I've got some cop friends. There's a safe house in—"

"No, don't give me the details," Kyle said. It was better that he didn't know so he wouldn't be tempted to find her.

They headed upstairs, Kyle steeling himself against Andrea's reaction. He'd have to be rude to her, maybe even cruel, to drive her away. He'd lie and say that what he and Andrea had shared was an act of desperation: two people thinking they were facing death and wanting to feel alive one last time.

And they had. And it was over.

A knot formed in his chest. Tom pushed open the door into the kitchen.

"I've got sandwiches—PB and J, ham, egg salad," Claudia said.

"Where's Andrea?" Kyle asked.

"Went to the garage for some granola bars and juice boxes."

Kyle strapped on the backpack. "Let me talk to her." Tom nodded in understanding.

Kyle smiled as he passed the kids playing on the kitchen floor. Tom didn't know how good he had it: children, a woman who loved him. Kyle would be turning his back on that possibility when he left here.

Damn, only then did he realize he'd gone to that place and had started fantasizing about a future with the woman. He opened the door to the garage. "Andrea?"

The garage was empty and the door open. No, this was not possible.

"Andrea!"

Tom raced into the garage. "What the…where is she?"

Chapter Fourteen

"That sonofabitch," Kyle said. "Biehl's got her. I was right downstairs. They wanted me. Why didn't they just take me?"

"I know I wasn't followed," Tom said. "How did they know she was here?"

Claudia poked her head into the garage. "What's going on?"

"Andrea's gone," Tom said.

"What? But—"

"What happened before she came out here?" Kyle asked.

"She answered the phone for me but it was a wrong number. Then she went to the garage to get supplies."

Kyle shared a knowing look with Tom. The phone call must have been Biehl threatening her family if she didn't come willingly. But why not take Kyle as well?

"Hang on, what's that?" Tom pointed to a piece of paper in the wiper blade of his car. Kyle snapped it free and opened the note.

Wait for my call if you want her to live.

He crumpled it into a ball and leaned against the car. "Damn it."

"Where would he take her?"

Kyle didn't want to speculate on that one. If Biehl took her to The Lab... No, Kyle wouldn't lose her like this.

"Do you have a cell phone?" Kyle asked.

Tom pulled it from his belt and handed it to him. Kyle slipped the private number from his wallet and made the call.

"Crane," a man answered.

"It's Kyle McKendrick. Biehl's taken her, do you know where?"

"Honey, I told you before, I can't get a leave to take the kids to the cabin. There just isn't time right now."

"Biehl's taken her back to her cabin?"

"Yes... Okay, then we'll talk later."

Kyle hung up and looked at Tom. "Get yourself and your family to a safe house. Give me your cell-phone number. If you don't hear from me by tomorrow noon, contact Lieutenant Crane at this number." He scribbled Crane's number on the back of Biehl's note. "Tell him you've got the evidence against Major Biehl."

He handed Tom half a dozen photos from the envelope and kept the rest.

"I'm coming with you," Tom said.

"You need to take care of your family. This is all that's left of Jimmy, you guys." He hesitated. "And Andrea."

"You really care about her."

"More than she'll ever know."

Tom fished keys out of his pocket. "Take the minivan,

and do the one thing I never could. Take care of my sister-in-law."

"Count on it.

HOURS LATER Kyle hid the van in a cluster of trees a safe distance from the cabin. Using the natural terrain as cover, he discreetly took out the two soldiers positioned at the top of the drive. Luckily the sun had set and darkness blanketed the camp below. A fire burned in the pit. Two other soldiers sipped from tin mugs, occasionally glancing up as the sounds of nature drew their attention.

Kyle shifted into the thick mass of a pine and hunkered down for a better look. He eyed Andrea's cabin and spotted Biehl pacing the main room, waving his hands and shouting.

Where was she? Had he already killed her?

A sharp pain lanced his chest. *Focus, soldier, focus.*

He shot a flare across the soldiers' line of vision. They jumped up, guns aimed into the darkness. Biehl came out of the cabin, dragging Andrea by the arm. She looked tired and beaten. As though she'd given up. But she was alive.

Anger burned Kyle's insides. He edged his way around to the other side of the camp.

"McKendrick! Is that you?" Biehl called. "I'm ready to make a trade. Your life for this woman." Biehl said something to the soldiers and they disappeared into the surrounding brush.

"She's a beauty!" Biehl called.

Don't let him get to you, Mac.

"Bet she tastes good, too!"

Kyle shoved back his temper. "Go ahead and try, bastard," he whispered.

Stay focused.

He concentrated on the soldier heading his way. About twenty feet out. Fifteen. Kyle slowed his breathing, ignored Biehl, and waited until the soldier was within range.

"I think she likes me, McKendrick! I think she's already forgotten about you."

The soldier slowed as if he sensed Kyle's presence.

"C'mon, Andy, let's you and me go in the cabin where we can have some privacy," Biehl called out.

With a steadying breath, Kyle sprang up and threw a knife directly into the soldier's back. He grunted and fell to the ground.

"I bet she's a real hellion in bed, McKendrick. Mind if I give her a ride?"

Kyle crouched down and waited for the second soldier's approach. When the soldier found his dead partner, he kneeled to examine the injury, then suddenly jumped up, realizing his mistake.

"Wrong move, soldier." Kyle choked him unconscious and hid him out of sight.

"McKendrick? I know you're out there," Biehl called to the mountains.

He marched onto the property. "You're right, of course, Major, like always."

Biehl spun around.

"And we're all alone," Kyle said, his voice thick with challenge.

Biehl scanned the area and pulled out his radio. "Edwards? Langdon? What's your position? Over."

"Their position is flat on the ground, sir," Kyle said.

"You're quite the soldier." Biehl holstered his radio and started down the steps, using Andrea as a shield. When he got to the bottom of the stairs, he pulled his pistol from his belt and pointed it to the back of her head.

Kyle's blood pressure spiked.

"Toss your weapons by the fire," Biehl ordered.

"I thought this was going to be a fair fight."

"It will be, son. It will be."

Kyle tossed his two pistols and knife to the ground. "So," he said, stepping around the campfire to get a better shot at the major. "It's just you and me."

"Ah…but let's not forget our friend here. She's been quite good company, haven't you?" Biehl tugged on her hair and Andrea whimpered.

Then he kissed her. She hammered at his chest with closed fists. Kyle reined in the emotions that threatened to send him flying across the fire at Biehl.

"C'mon, Major. I thought you'd outgrown molesting women. She only complicates things. Let her go and let's you and me finish this."

"You'd like that, wouldn't you? To finally get a piece of me?"

"Who says I'd get a piece of you? You taught me everything I know."

"Including humility," Biehl said.

Kyle smiled and fought to ignore Andrea's panicked expression. His feelings for her would only weaken him.

"This should be fun, McKendrick. But first, we need to figure out where this bitch's husband hid the evidence against me."

"That's easy." He kneeled and pulled off his backpack.

"Careful there." Biehl pressed the gun to Andrea's temple.

"But I found the evidence, sir."

Biehl shot him a look of disbelief. "Are you trying to trick me, soldier?"

"No, sir. The evidence was in Jimmy's brother's basement. Photographs of Beta Force missions gone bad."

"Toss it over."

"Let her go first."

"I'm not a fool." Biehl pulled her closer to him. The once bright-green of her eyes had faded to a dull gray, lit only by the reflection of the burning fire. "Toss the evidence to the ground where I can see it."

"Kyle, don't," she said.

Kyle was startled by the intensity of her voice. "Don't lose this way," she said. "Not to him."

"Shut up! A simple squeeze of my finger and you're dead." Biehl threatened. "Is that what you want?" he shrieked.

She closed her eyes as if she'd accepted her fate.

"How about an even exchange?" Kyle asked. "The evidence for Andrea's life. Let her go and keep me."

Biehl's eyes brightened. "Fine. But she leaves after I've inspected the evidence."

Kyle knew what that meant: no one was getting out of here alive.

Biehl shoved her to the ground between them and Kyle automatically stepped forward.

"Not yet, McKendrick. The evidence." He motioned with his fingers.

Kyle glanced at Andrea, who seemed frozen in place. He tossed the pictures to the ground. "It's all there."

Biehl eyed the gruesome shots. "Pick those up and bring them to me, Andy."

As she reached for the photographs, Kyle recognized the horror in her eyes at what she saw there. Yep, that's what Kyle and Jimmy were about: killing, maiming. Shame coursed through his body. Then she glanced up at him, her eyes filled with sympathy.

No, it wasn't possible.

She was a healer, a woman determined to save the people she loved. Kyle wasn't redeemable, and yet he knew that if they survived this she'd spend her life trying to save him.

He loved her too much to chain her to this ugliness. He'd have to let her go, even after he saved her life. He had to give her a chance at a pleasant life with a gentle, stable man who wasn't haunted by a gruesome past and countless sins.

Andrea handed the pictures to Biehl. His eyes lit up as he studied the photographs. "Hmmm. Yes, this was one of my favorite missions."

"You've got what you want. Let her go. It's over." Kyle started toward Andrea.

"Over?" Biehl said, pulling a knife from his belt and holding it against her throat. "Not yet. See, she wants to hear what a hero her husband was, how much he loved his work, the killing, the torture, having sex with strangers to get information out of them. He was a good boy. A very good boy. Not like McKendrick here."

"You sonofa—"

"Watch it!" Biehl warned, the knife's edge drawing a trickle of blood from Andrea's skin. "McKendrick taught your husband everything, and then killed him."

Kyle fisted his hands. He'd kill this man if it was the last thing he did on this earth.

ANDREA KNEW it was a lie, but if she acted the part of vengeful wife it might buy Kyle some time to get the advantage.

"And now this murderer wants you, sweet Andrea, because of some misguided sense of honor I suppose," Biehl said. "He probably thinks if you forgive him, that makes everything all right. Do you? Do you forgive him?"

"I could never forgive him," she lied.

Don't listen to my words. See into my heart, my love.

Kyle's expression hardened and his eyes grew dark.

Biehl loosened his grip and she knew she'd done the right thing. "Don't worry, I'll avenge Jimmy's death for you," Biehl whispered against her ear. "First, I'll have a little fun with him. I'll aim for that shoulder wound of his to bring him to his knees. Once he's down I'll slash his face, the same face that's haunted me for weeks."

Kyle didn't move.

"Bloody red," Biehl continued. "That's how this boy will look after I'm done." Andrea started to squirm. "What's the matter, Andy? I'm going to destroy your husband's murderer. That's what you want, isn't it?"

"Of course," she lied, her heart a roller coaster of emotion. She ached to wipe that expression off Kyle's face; she ached to be in his arms. She loved him. And she knew he loved her.

They both love me, it's only right that they take care of each other. Jimmy's words.

"Let the fun begin!" Biehl tied her to a nearby tree, keeping his eyes trained on Kyle. "All right, boy," Biehl said, stalking to Kyle. "It's you and me."

She pulled on her bindings.

"Look at that. She wants to help. Sorry, Andy, but this one's all mine."

Kyle dove at Biehl and they hit the ground, scrambling for the dominant position. They jumped to their feet, ready for the next round. Biehl delivered a kick to Kyle's stomach but Kyle recovered and knocked Biehl to the ground with a smack to the jaw. Kyle pinned Biehl, and Andrea breathed a sigh of relief. But Biehl punched Kyle in the shoulder wound.

Kyle jerked back in pain and collapsed.

Biehl pulled off his belt.

"Didn't your daddy ever take a strap to you, boy? I'll bet he did." Biehl jerked his wrist and the snap of his belt cracked against the wind. "Did he whip you for not remembering to take the car in for repairs? I'll bet he beat you good for what you did to your sister."

"Damn you!" Kyle charged.

She tugged on her ropes, trying not to watch as Biehl thrashed at Kyle. But her eyes were drawn to the scene, her heart crumbling with each failed attempt by Kyle to knock Biehl down.

"It was all your fault, wasn't it?" Biehl taunted, as Kyle came after him again, only to have the leather belt sear through his shirt and slice his skin. Kyle charged five times, each time Biehl drawing new blood somewhere on Kyle's body.

"Fight like a man, you worthless old bastard," Kyle taunted, his breathing heavy, blood spotting his chest, his upper arms and his left cheek.

"I've got a lot more, McKendrick." Biehl tossed the belt to the ground.

She couldn't stand feeling so helpless. Biehl closed in for the kill and her heart pounded. She loved Kyle. And it didn't matter.

Kyle dodged Biehl's first punch. They scrambled and rolled in a blur of motion. One minute Kyle was on top hammering away, the next, Biehl had Kyle by the shirt collar, banging his head against the ground.

"You're nothing but a coward. You've got no guts, no brains and no fighting strength. Look at you!" Biehl said in disgust, ramming his fist into Kyle's shoulder.

Biehl got up, and Kyle rolled onto his side in agony, his expression a tormented plea that made Andy pull harder on her ropes. He'd tried and failed. Now they were both going to die.

"You're a loser, McKendrick, a damned loser," Biehl said, punctuating each word with a kick to Kyle's midsection.

"Stop!" Andrea cried out, staring at Kyle's limp body.

Biehl turned to her. "Why? This is the man who killed your husband. Isn't this what he deserves?"

She looked desperately at Kyle. His eyes were closed, his arms protectively wrapped around his middle.

"I…"

"What? You want it over quick or do you want me to brutalize the man like he brutalized your husband? Go on, speak up."

She caught the look in Biehl's eyes. He'd slipped over the edge, she could tell by the maniacal glint, the strained curve of his lips. She pulled on her bindings as Biehl closed in.

"You're not afraid of me, are you?" Biehl said. "I haven't properly thanked you for helping me bring in my renegade agent. Without you as bait, McKendrick would have disappeared again."

He edged closer and there was nowhere to go. Her heart pounded, her thoughts raced. "No," she muttered, as he reached out to touch her cheek.

Out of the corner of her eye, she saw a flash of gold as her golden retriever attacked Biehl. He went down before he could pull his gun.

"Oscar," she hushed. He must have left the Simpson ranch to search for Andrea.

Biehl swore and fought to rid himself of the stubborn retriever. But Oscar's teeth held firmly to the man's arm.

"My turn!" Kyle said, pushing Oscar aside. "I should kill you, you sonofabitch!" Kyle cried, pummeling Biehl's face with his fists.

She watched as Kyle released his rage on the major. She should have been horrified at his behavior, but Andrea, of all people, understood the need for justice.

Biehl stopped moving, stopped fighting. She watched

the play of emotions cross Kyle's face: anger, embarrassment and relief. His breathing was heavy, his savage eyes on fire; she didn't know what to say to calm him, to tell him it was over, that he could finally let go.

Kyle climbed off Biehl and went to her. He framed her cheeks with his steady hands and reached over to untie her wrists.

Oscar growled and the hair pricked on the back of her neck. She glanced over Kyle's shoulder to see Biehl stumbling toward them.

"Kyle!"

He jumped to his feet and charged Biehl, who was aiming a gun at them. A shot rang out, then two more.

"No!" She pulled on her bindings.

"You?" Biehl said.

She spotted Lieutenant Crane in the distance, aiming a rifle at Biehl. Biehl crumbled to his knees, gripping his chest.

Kyle was sprawled on the ground, motionless.

"No, Kyle, untie me, someone untie me," she cried.

"Get the major into the truck," Crane ordered his men. They dragged Biehl away from the scene. Then Crane kneeled beside Kyle and leaned close, as if to determine whether he was breathing.

With an open palm to Kyle's chest, Lieutenant Crane bowed his head.

"No, he's alive, I know he's alive," she said.

Lieutenant Crane stood and faced her. "I'm sorry."

And once again, her world was ripped apart.

Chapter Fifteen

It was the right thing to do, Kyle thought, splitting another piece of wood. His injury ached in protest. He'd better take it easy.

Not like leaving Andrea two months ago had been easy. She'd practically attached herself to Kyle's supposedly dead body, demanding that she be allowed to try her own brand of healing to bring him back to life.

Every night as he lay in bed, her cries echoed in his brain, taunting him, scolding him. How could he break her heart like that? Playing dead had been the best way to break the bond between them.

Who was he kidding? He still dreamt of her, imagined her lavender scent and sparkling green eyes. She'd haunt him until his last day on earth.

He glanced at the sky. Another day of overcast and drizzle in the Pacific Northwest. He'd been reborn in a rugged part of Oregon, bought a cabin with cash and planned to spend the next few years recovering from his life. He'd never recover from loving Andrea, and that was his penance. He wouldn't be selfish and invite her into his unpredictable life. He owed her her freedom.

He swung the ax down on another piece of wood. His shoulder wound ached. Good, maybe it would distract him from the ache in his heart.

A dark blue Suburban with tinted windows turned down his long drive. Not good. That usually related to the government assignments he'd hoped to forget. The car pulled up to the house and Crane got out.

"Lieutenant," Kyle said, saluting.

Crane extended his hand. "We're past that, Kyle."

They shook hands. "Should I be worried about this unexpected visit?" Kyle said.

"Just wanted to give you an update." He'd driven all the way out here to give Kyle an update? Something was up.

"Biehl's been taken care of, quietly, and the men have been debriefed. The military is keeping this an internal investigation."

"I figured as much."

"Beta Force started off right, it just got perverted by the major's ego. We uncovered the truth about Jimmy Franks's death."

Kyle held his breath.

"Biehl had him shot, but you didn't do it. You had most of the story correct. The major set him up to die at the hands of terrorists. The chopper took off and you lost your mind. A soldier knocked you out and was ordered to shoot Jimmy. They changed that last part for you, so Biehl could keep you in line."

"Bastard," Kyle whispered.

"Yep."

But Kyle had still lured Jimmy into Beta Force. He still felt responsible for his fate.

"You didn't answer my question," Kyle said. "Should I be worried about this unexpected visit?"

"I don't know, should you?" He motioned toward the truck. The door opened and Andrea climbed out.

The wind ripped from his chest. "What is she doing here?"

"She's my last assignment."

Kyle snapped his attention to Crane.

"There's been so much devastation thanks to Biehl," Crane said. "Let's end this thing right. She loves you, McKendrick. Don't let Biehl ruin that, too."

"You shouldn't have brought her here." Kyle's heart raced. Just looking at her made him feel alive again.

Andrea walked up to him. "So here's the coward," she challenged.

"Well, I'll leave you two lovebirds alone." Crane went to the car.

"Wait a second," Kyle protested. "You can't leave her here."

Then she touched his face and turned him to look at her. God, she looked beautiful, her emerald eyes sparkling with love.

For Kyle.

"You shouldn't be here," he said. "You know what I am."

"A hero who saved my life."

"Don't romanticize this, Andrea. I'm—"

"A caring man who carries so much guilt on his shoulders. An honorable man who would have sacrificed his life to save young soldiers." She leaned forward and kissed his cheek. "A gentle, tender lover," she whispered.

And he lost himself. "This can never be," he said, his voice hoarse.

"Sure it can."

Suddenly the two golden retrievers jumped out of the car and came running up to them. She leaned back and looked into his eyes. "Crane is right. Our best revenge is to be happy. To be in love."

"I…Jimmy," he choked.

"It's time to move on, to forgive yourself. I need you."

I need you. Hope soared through his chest. The queen of independence admitted she needed him.

"You…need me?"

"Sure," she said with a grin. "I was never any good at splitting wood."

"Oh, so it's brute strength you're after."

"That," she said, placing an open palm against his chest. "And a warm heart."

"The heart's yours," he whispered. "But the brute strength, it might be a while before I'm up to a lot of manual labor."

"That's okay, McKendrick," she said, stroking his cheek. "I've got all the time in the world."

* * * * *

Look for LAST WOLF WATCHING
by Rhyannon Byrd—the exciting conclusion in the
BLOODRUNNERS *miniseries*
from Silhouette Nocturne.

Follow Michaela and Brody on their fierce journey
to find the truth and face the demons from the past,
as they reach the heart of the battle between the
Runners and the rogues.

Here is a sneak preview of book three,
LAST WOLF WATCHING.

covered bodies standing like monstrous shadows at the

Michaela squinted, struggling to see through the impenetrable darkness. Everyone looked toward the Elders, but she knew Brody Carter still watched her. Michaela could feel the power of his gaze. Its heat. Its strength. And something that felt strangely like anger, though he had no reason to have any emotion toward her. Strangers from different worlds, brought together beneath the heavy silver moon on a night made for hell itself. That was their only connection.

The second she finished that thought, she knew it was a lie. But she couldn't deal with it now. Not tonight. Not when her whole world balanced on the edge of destruction.

Willing her backbone to keep her upright, Michaela Doucet focused on the towering blaze of a roaring bonfire that rose from the far side of the clearing, its orange flames burning with maniacal zeal against the inky black curtain of the night. Many of the Lycans had already shifted into their preternatural shapes, their fur-covered bodies standing like monstrous shadows at the

edges of the forest as they waited with restless expec-
tancy for her brother.

Her nineteen-year-old brother, Max, had been
attacked by a rogue werewolf—a Lycan who preyed
upon humans for food. Max had been bitten in the attack,
which meant he was no longer human, but a breed of
creature that existed between the two worlds of man
and beast, much like the Bloodrunners themselves.

The Elders parted, and two hulking shapes emerged
from the trees. In their wolf forms, the Lycans stood
over seven feet tall, their legs bent at an odd angle as
they stalked forward. They each held a thick chain that
had been wound around their inside wrists, the twin
lengths leading back into the shadows. The Lycans had
taken no more than a few steps when they jerked on the
chains, and her brother appeared.

Bound like an animal.

Biting at her trembling lower lip, she glanced left,
then right, surprised to see that others had joined her.
Now the Bloodrunners and their family and friends stood
as a united force against the Silvercrest pack, which had
yet to accept the fact that something sinister was eating
away at its foundation—something that would rip down
the protective walls that separated their world from the
humans'. It occurred to Michaela that loyalties were
being announced tonight—a separation made between
those who would stand with the Runners in their fight
against the rogues and those who blindly supported the
pack's refusal to face reality. But all she could focus on
was her brother. Max looked so hurt…so terrified.

"Leave him alone," she screamed, her soft-soled,

black satin slip-ons struggling for purchase in the damp earth as she rushed toward Max, only to find herself lifted off the ground when a hard, heavily muscled arm clamped around her waist from behind, pulling her clear off her feet. "Damn it, let me down!" she snarled, unable to take her eyes off her brother as the golden-eyed Lycan kicked him.

Mindless with heartache and rage, Michaela clawed at the arm holding her, kicking her heels against whatever part of her captor's legs she could reach. "Stop it," a deep, husky voice grunted in her ear. "You're not helping him by losing it. I give you my word he'll survive the ceremony, but you have to keep it together."

"Nooooo!" she screamed, too hysterical to listen to reason. "You're monsters! All of you! Look what you've done to him! How dare you! *How dare you!*"

The arm tightened with a powerful flex of muscle, cinching her waist. Her breath sucked in on a sharp, wailing gasp.

"Shut up before you get both yourself and your brother killed. I will *not* let that happen. Do you understand me?" her captor growled, shaking her so hard that her teeth clicked together. "Do you understand me, Doucet?"

"Damn it," she cried, stricken as she watched one of the guards grab Max by his hair. Around them Lycans huffed and growled as they watched the spectacle, while others outright howled for the show to begin.

"That's enough!" the voice seethed in her ear. "They'll tear you apart before you even reach him, and I'll be damned if I'm going to stand here and watch you die."

Suddenly, through the haze of fear and agony and

outrage in her mind, she finally recognized who'd caught her. *Brody*.

He held her in his arms, her body locked against his powerful form, her back to the burning heat of his chest. A low, keening sound of anguish tore through her, and her head dropped forward as hoarse sobs of pain ripped from her throat. "Let me go. I have to help him. *Please*," she begged brokenly, knowing only that she needed to get to Max. "Let me go, Brody."

He muttered something against her hair, his breath warm against her scalp, and Michaela could have sworn it was a single word…. But she must have heard wrong. She was too upset. Too furious. Too terrified. She must be out of her mind.

Because it sounded as if he'd quietly snarled the word *never*.

nocturne™

THE FINAL INSTALLMENT OF THE BLOODRUNNERS TRILOGY

Last Wolf Watching

Runner Brody Carter has found his match in Michaela Doucet, a human with unusual psychic powers. When Michaela's brother is threatened, Brody becomes her protector, and suddenly not only has to protect her from her enemies but also from himself....

LOOK FOR

LAST WOLF WATCHING
BY
RHYANNON BYRD

Available May 2008 wherever you buy books.

Dramatic and Sensual Tales of Paranormal Romance

SPECIAL EDITION™

 THE WILDER FAMILY
Healing Hearts in Walnut River

Social worker Isobel Suarez was proud to
work at Walnut River General Hospital, so
when Neil Kane showed up from the attorney
general's office to investigate insurance fraud,
she was up in arms. Until she melted in his
arms, and things got very tricky...

Look for

HER MR. RIGHT?
by
KAREN ROSE SMITH

Available May wherever books are sold.

Silhouette®

Romantic
SUSPENSE

**Sparked by Danger,
Fueled by Passion.**

Seduction Summer:
Seduction in the sand...and a killer on the beach.

*Silhouette Romantic Suspense invites you to the hottest
summer yet with three connected stories from some
of our steamiest storytellers! Get ready for...*

Killer Temptation
by Nina Bruhns;
a millionaire this tempting is worth a little danger.

Killer Passion
by Sheri WhiteFeather;
an FBI profiler's forbidden passion incites a
killer's rage,

and

Killer Affair
by Cindy Dees;
this affair with a mystery man is to die for.

Look for

KILLER TEMPTATION by Nina Bruhns in June 2008
KILLER PASSION by Sheri WhiteFeather in July 2008
and
KILLER AFFAIR by Cindy Dees in August 2008.

Available wherever you buy books!

HARLEQUIN

More Than Words

"There are moms. There are angels. And then there's Sally."

—**Kathleen O'Brien**, author

Kathleen wrote "Step by Step," inspired by Sally Hanna-Schaefer, founder of **Mother/Child Residential Program,** *where for over twenty-six years Sally has provided support for pregnant women and women with children.*

Look for "*Step by Step*" in
More Than Words, Vol. 4,
available in April 2008 at eHarlequin.com
or wherever books are sold.

SUPPORTING CAUSES OF CONCERN TO WOMEN ‖ HARLEQUIN
WWW.HARLEQUINMORETHANWORDS.COM

MTW07SH2

REQUEST YOUR FREE BOOKS!

2 FREE NOVELS PLUS 2 FREE GIFTS!

HARLEQUIN®

INTRIGUE®

Breathtaking Romantic Suspense

YES! Please send me 2 FREE Harlequin Intrigue® novels and my 2 FREE gifts (gifts are worth about $10). After receiving them, if I don't wish to receive any more books, I can return the shipping statement marked "cancel." If I don't cancel, I will receive 6 brand-new novels every month and be billed just $4.24 per book in the U.S. or $4.99 per book in Canada, plus 25¢ shipping and handling per book and applicable taxes, if any*. That's a savings of close to 15% off the cover price! I understand that accepting the 2 free books and gifts places me under no obligation to buy anything. I can always return a shipment and cancel at any time. Even if I never buy another book from Harlequin, the two free books and gifts are mine to keep forever.

182 HDN EEZ7   382 HDN EEZK

Name _____ (PLEASE PRINT) _____

Address _____ Apt. # _____

City _____ State/Prov. _____ Zip/Postal Code _____

Signature (if under 18, a parent or guardian must sign)

Mail to the **Harlequin Reader Service:**
IN U.S.A.: P.O. Box 1867, Buffalo, NY 14240-1867
IN CANADA: P.O. Box 609, Fort Erie, Ontario L2A 5X3

Not valid to current subscribers of Harlequin Intrigue books.

Want to try two free books from another line?
Call 1-800-873-8635 or visit www.morefreebooks.com.

* Terms and prices subject to change without notice. N.Y. residents add applicable sales tax. Canadian residents will be charged applicable provincial taxes and GST. This offer is limited to one order per household. All orders subject to approval. Credit or debit balances in a customer's account(s) may be offset by any other outstanding balance owed by or to the customer. Please allow 4 to 6 weeks for delivery. Offer available while quantities last.

Your Privacy: Harlequin is committed to protecting your privacy. Our Privacy Policy is available online at www.eHarlequin.com or upon request from the Reader Service. From time to time we make our lists of customers available to reputable third parties who may have a product or service of interest to you. If you would prefer we not share your name and address, please check here. ☐

NEW YORK TIMES BESTSELLING AUTHOR
SHARON SALA

All his life, Jonah Gray Wolf has had an uncanny connection
to animals, and the power to heal the sick and wounded.
Driven from the only home he's ever known by those who
wish to harness his gift for profit, he becomes a drifter. It's a
lonely life, but Jonah knows he's still being hunted....

In West Virginia, he finds Luce—a kindred soul with whom
he might dare to make a life. But danger is coming to
their mountain refuge—a confrontation that will be
decided only by a force of nature.

THE
HEALER

"(Sharon Sala) takes readers with her on an incredible
journey."—John St. Augustine, Host, *Power! Talk Radio*

Available the first week of April 2008 wherever books are sold!

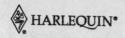

HARLEQUIN®

INTRIGUE®

COMING NEXT MONTH

#1059 SECOND CHANCE COWBOY by B.J. Daniels
Whitehorse, Montana

Arlene Evans didn't believe she deserved a second chance. But then Hank Monroe entered her life. Together they searched for Arlene's missing daughter, only to discover it's never too late to fall in love.

#1060 COLD CASE CONNECTION by Kathleen Long
The Body Hunters

Lily Christides never imagined she'd one day be chasing her sister's killer, but only Cameron Hughes had the skills to aid her investigation. The devoted detective knew all too well the high cost of truth—and redemption.

#1061 TWIN TARGETS by Jessica Andersen
Thriller

Sidney Westlake would do anything to save her twin sister—even if it brought her on the wrong side of the law. Could Special Agent John Sharpe set her straight—or would both she and her sister pay the price?

#1062 WITH THE MATERIAL WITNESS IN THE SAFE HOUSE by Carla Cassidy
The Curse of Raven's Cliff

A quaint seaside village's most chilling secrets are revealed for the first time in this new continuity! Britta Jakobsen disappeared from the witness protection program without a trace. But could Ryan Burton return Britta to safety—when the most dangerous thing in her life was him?

#1063 IN THE FLESH by Rita Herron
Nighthawk Island

Jenny Madden did nothing but get under Detective Raul Cortez's skin. But the psychiatrist was the latest target of a deranged killer, and all personal feelings aside, she needed his protection. But the silk strangler might not be the last man to take her breath away....

#1064 STARGAZER'S WOMAN by Aimée Thurlo
Brotherhood of Warriors

Was Max Natoni a stargazer—a Navajo with the special ability to find that which is lost? All it's done so far is lead him to Kristin Reynolds, a marine looking for a killer. Can the two solve the crime before it gets them more than they're looking for?

www.eHarlequin.com

HICNM0408